BACHELOR BOSS

SARA NEY

1

PHILLIP

"I swear to God, Humphrey, if you don't take a piss soon, I'm going to stop bringing you to the dog park," I threaten as my dog takes his sweet-ass time, sniffing bushes and fences and the concrete sidewalk.

He's supposed to be peeing.

Humphrey has other ideas.

Never one to take direction or learn obedience, my Basset Hound meanders at a glacially slow pace, taking up most of the sidewalk with his wide ass. He halts, wags his tail, then goes still again.

Fuck, he sees something; now there's no way he's going to listen.

The little bastard strains against his leash, gagging and choking and gasping for air as if I'm the one yanking on him and not the other way around.

Gag.

Cough.

Could he be any more dramatic?

"Come on dude, go potty. It's freezing out here."

Thing is—he doesn't actually *know* any commands, though not for lack of trying on my part. I've taken Humphrey to training several times with little luck. For a Basset Hound—a dog with a supposedly even and mild temper—he's inopportunely stubborn. Humphrey occasionally responds to one command and one command only:

Lay down.

Know why? Because he's always laying down.

"Go potty," I tell him again.

Humphrey does not go potty.

"Dammit! I'm serious. Go. Potty." Now I'm getting stern, infusing my tone with discipline so he knows I mean business.

The dog wags his tail.

"No, stop it." I point to the spot on the ground I believe would be a fantastic location for him to take a piss. "I said go potty."

We continue like this until I'm good and late for work, the dog begrudgingly walking and peeing at the same time, not bothering to stop or lift his leg while we make our way back to my house. I live in a brownstone in an up-and-coming area of Chicago that's great for families because, to be honest, I thought I'd have one by now.

I've had a few steady girlfriends, despite them all discovering I'm not their soul mate and dumping me for another man. At the ripe old age of twenty-eight, it's discouraging, but that hasn't stopped me from looking for The One. Or hoping for The One. She hasn't shown up on my doorstep, so instead of dating, I'm carrying not the toddler I thought I'd have by now, but an ungrateful dog up the stairs to my front door, because the shithead refused to budge from sniffing crap in the shrubberies outside.

Nosey turd.

"You made me late for work." He wags that outlandishly long tail again as I scratch behind his floppy ears, watching with satisfaction as he savors the feeling of my nails against his skin. Fur. Whatever. "You always make me late," I lecture, softening my tone.

It's a fact, and not a fun one.

It's also a fact that I could probably wake up earlier every morning, but instead, I hit snooze to snooze and snooze and snooze, both the dog and me dozing and dozing and dozing longer than we should.

Making sure the dog is situated, I thumb through the apps on my phone, find the one for a car, tap, swipe to confirm. Race around my place, locking up, shutting off lights, and bound back down the stairs to head to work.

* * *

"You're late."

The hall monitor of our office doesn't glance up from his desk, inconveniently located in the first cubicle on the block, his chair swiveling in my direction as my feet hit the smooth, cold, marble floor in the lobby.

I haven't even stepped four feet inside the place and Paul Danbury is riding my ass. He's not actually a hall monitor, simply someone who won't mind his own business. What Paul *is* is an executive assistant who hasn't learned that monitoring employee comings and goings, tardiness, or absences *is not his job*. That's my boss's job, and last time I checked, her name isn't Paul—it's Patrice.

"You're late," he says again, as if I didn't hear him the first time.

I barely conceal a sneer. "Really? You think I didn't know that?"

"I mean—it's not a great way to start the week."

"What's your point?"

"Last week you were late twice."

I try to walk past him without commenting, really I do. But Paul is neither my boss nor human resources, and this is none of his damn business.

So I don't walk past him. I swivel on my heel, look him in the eye, and, like a grown-up, say, "So?"

"It's a bad habit to get into." Great. The last thing I need is Paul reporting me to management, or HR, or someone else in the office who has a grudge against me—I'm sure there are plenty who would love to see my ass get canned.

"No, *smoking* is a bad habit to get into. I have a dog that doesn't listen to jack shit, including me."

Paul sits up straighter in his chair, interested. "What kind of dog?"

Oh, Paul likes animals?

Fantastic.

If chatting about my lazy-ass pup is going to get my late ass out of trouble, I'll lean into it. Resting my elbow on the top of Paul's cubicle wall, I sigh dramatically—just like Humphrey would do.

"A Basset Hound. He has behavioral issues."

The issue is: he doesn't behave and lords it over me every waking minute of the day. For such a gangly and awkward animal, he sure is a dickhead.

"Oh my God, I love Basset Hounds," Paul drawls out with a swoon. "Does he have those big floppy ears?"

"Yeah." They're floppy all right. I pull my cell phone out of my back pocket and click open the photo gallery. I have an embarrassing abundance of Humphrey pictures on my phone—more than any self-respecting man should have of a dog who won't smile for the camera or make eye contact with it, either. "Want to see a picture of him?"

Paul nods. Fervently.

Cool.

I swipe through, ashamed of the sheer number of selfies I've taken with my dog, some with filters, some without, all with Humphrey's lack of motivation.

"OMG this one of him with Santa—I want to die." Paul clutches his chest as if it's just too much for him to bear, this photo of my dog with Santa Claus at the fake North Pole. Inside the mall.

Yeah. I still can't believe I took him to see Santa.

In my defense, my sister thought it would be cute, and she was in town visiting, so did I actually have a choice, or was I a victim of her sibling intimidation? She's older than me by two years and always tries to lord the power over me the same way the dog does.

"What's his name?" Paul asks after his fingers stop swiping across my screen. He props his chin in his other hand, settling into the subject.

"Humphrey."

Paul gasps. "It's too perfect. He looks like a Humphrey."

I relax my shoulders a little, the stress beginning to leave my body. Maybe Paul isn't such a prick after all, and maybe he won't say anything about me being late.

"What does he love?"

"Sleeping."

Paul chuckles as if it's the most amusing thing he's heard all morning. "What else?"

"Laying down."

Paul's brows go up. "What else?"

"Eating."

"Dang, you're making your dog sound like an unemployed bachelor who lives with his parents." He relinquishes my phone and slaps it back in my palm, satisfied.

"That's exactly what he is, a bachelor who lives at home with his one parent—me."

Paul laughs, and I take advantage of this leeway he's granted me, the parlay for freedom.

"He has a mind of his own. Try carrying a seventy-pound dog home from the dog park every morning because he won't pee and he won't budge, and is out of shape. Or he gets himself lost in the bushes on purpose." Then I add, "Maybe I'll bring him by sometime."

"Yes! Do it."

I shoot him a thumbs-up, hiking the computer bag higher on my shoulder, and shuffle toward my office.

My *office*.

After three years at this company, I've clawed my way to a corner—three years of kissing ass, busting my balls, and dealing with gossipy, backstabbing co-workers. Like Paul. Only today I was able to win him over with the help of my hound, who almost never comes in handy for *any*thing.

I round the corner, hang another left, and head toward the corridor of offices with the best city views, mine at the end, at the glorious far end.

I give a whistle of contentment, a pep in my step now that I've dodged the hall monitor, and give my door a nudge with the toe of my shoe, pushing it the rest of the way open. Shrug my bag into my chair, pull my laptop from its sleeve, and center it on the calendar lining my desktop.

Blue light computer glasses.

Charger.

Then, I do what I do every workday: head for the breakroom, hands stuffed into the pockets of my brown cords as I go to scavenge for a free meal and hot beverage. You know, like I'm homeless and don't have food at my disposal.

The room isn't empty—a lot of people work on this floor, and at all hours of the workday, I can always expect a few of them to be snacking on something. I would know because at all hours of the day, I've been known to meander in for food. Or a beverage. Or just for a break, since we're thirty stories up and it's hardly worth an elevator ride down to the street for a ten-minute breather. Or a street hot dog.

Not worth it.

I greet Martin Duffy from accounting, an older dude wearing a bright blue shirt and a hot pink tie. Pretty sure Martin is single and ready to mingle—like myself—and the company breakroom is a prime spot for Marty to be on the prowl for the various single ladies working at this company.

A veritable speed-dating pool for those so inclined and with the nerve to hit on someone at work.

Like Martin.

"Hey Marty." I greet him at the same time he exits the room, holding up his muffin as a salutation, cell phone now pressed to his ear. I open one cabinet after the next, searching for a mug, anything to put a bit of coffee in. Locate one in the very last cabinet.

Now here is the thing: I don't actually drink coffee. Can't stand the taste of it. Can't stand the smell.

What I *do* enjoy is the process of preparing it, pouring it, and standing with my hip against the counter holding a hot, steamy cup on a cold day.

Basically to put off working.

I pour myself a mug, relaxing idly, eyeing up the breakfast pastries laid out on the countertop, all brought in from a company that wants to secure our business. Schmoozing us.

We're a contracting firm specializing in residential and industrial complexes and communities—communities my good buddy Brooks, an architect, designs. It's my job to award contracts for subcontractors on the industrial side—electrical, plumbing, heating and air conditioning. The whole nine yards.

High-rise apartments. Skyscrapers. Renovations for entire city blocks.

I award the contracts.

I'm not the boss, but if I play my cards right and kiss all the right asses, maybe I will be one day.

I nab a bagel, set my coffee prop on the counter (I'm not going to drink it anyway), and root around in the refrigerator for cream cheese. *Cream cheese, cream cheese, where is the cream cheese...*

Possibly some jelly? I'm in the mood for something sweet, and I'm one of those weird foodies who has to eat in order: no lunch food before I've had breakfast, no cake before lunch. Donuts, in my opinion, equal cake.

And today I'm friggin' starving enough to eat actual cake for breakfast, just watch me.

It takes some digging, but on the top shelf near the way way back, I find the cream cheese. Turn the container this way and that to find the expiration date. It's expired, but only by three weeks, so I crack the top and stick my nose in it, giving it a whiff.

My nose wrinkles the smallest bit. I mean, it smells kind of rank, but what are the chances it will actually make me sick?

Digging around for a knife, I stab it into the cream cheese and stir a bit to make it soft, the way I do at home, and—

"You're *not* seriously going to eat that are you?"

Glancing up, I see a girl—young woman, to be precise—leaning against the doorframe of the breakroom, sizing me up, mouth twisted into a curve of distaste. Pointedly glancing from me to the cream cheese container I'm holding in my hand, knife in the other.

I lift them both toward her and shrug. "I'm hungry."

"Enough to eat *expired* cream cheese?"

"How did you know it was expired?"

"Well, first I saw you check for the date, then I saw you sniff it—if it wasn't expired, you would have gone straight for a knife without doing a sniff test."

A sniff test. I hadn't realized that's what I was doing, but damn, she's right. It did stink and I probably shouldn't eat it—but what business is it of hers what I eat?

I don't know her; does she even work here? For all I know she's the muffin girl dropping off baked goods, or a subcontractor dropping off a bid.

"Right." I ignore her—she's not anyone I've ever met, no one I have to report to or worry about, but she is still staring at me. So I ignore her.

Although…to be fair, she *is* pretty damn attractive, so I'm not exactly mad about it.

Dark hair, dark blue eyes, curious stare.

I can *feel* her inspecting me as I smear the white-yellowish spread onto one half of my plain, untoasted bagel. A sad replacement for a donut, but I'll survive.

"You're not going to put that in the toaster?" She slowly comes toward me to watch.

"Nope." Not with her standing there not-so-silently judging everything I do.

Now she's at the fridge, leaning in. Reaches in and retrieves a carton of orange juice, fiddling with the twist top as I stir the cream cheese a little longer, lingering.

"Time for mimosas so early in the day?" I jest, creaming a second slice of bagel.

She semi-ignores me, grabbing a cup from a cabinet. "I would love a mimosa. I'll just have to pretend, won't I?" The girl pours, still not looking directly at me—but I do catch her side glance my way once or twice as I snatch a paper towel, wrapping my breakfast for takeaway.

Mmm mmm *good*.

"You're not going to eat it? Not going to take a bite *now*?" Still not looking at me.

"I will when I get to my desk."

Pouring herself a glass of OJ, she takes her sweet time, filling the entire cup with tart, orange liquid. Sips the top off and smiles. "I want to actually see you take a bite."

"Why?"

She raises those dark brows at me and smirks. Gives me a jaunty chin lift. "Go on, take a bite."

Well shit, now it's a matter of principle. She can't tell me what to do—*she is not the boss of me.*

I study her back critically. "What did you say your name is?"

"I didn't." Her arms cross, the cup of orange juice propped in one hand. "Take a bite."

"Stop being so bossy."

"I want to see if you'll gag. That's all. No big deal."

If I *gag*? "Why would I gag?"

"Why would you gag? Are you being for real right now?" A look of exasperation and incredulousness crosses her pretty face. "That spread you just wiped on your bagel is a thousand years old."

I barely contain my ire. "Over-exaggerate much?"

She gives me a one-shoulder shrug, waiting, still standing there, juice in hand. Daring me to bite into the bagel.

"Must be nice not to be in any rush and have nowhere to go in the middle of the workday," I smart at her, annoyed.

The young woman smiles. "It really is."

She's being sarcastic and I don't appreciate it, mostly because suddenly, I can smell the rancid cheese caked on my breakfast unwelcomely wafting into my nostrils. Notice for the first time the crust crystalized on the edge of one dollop.

Fuck.

The girl gives me a knowing smile—she fucking *knows* I *know*.

Her smile is megawatt. "Is something amiss?"

Amiss? Yes, something is a-fucking-miss.

"Nope."

She sips her juice again, slurping loudly and smiling over the brim of her cup. That knowing knowingness.

It's infuriating.

But I can't just chuck the damn bagel in the trash—cannot give her the satisfaction of being right, this girl I do not know and have never met.

She needs to go away so I can throw this thing in the trash and figure out what I am going to eat. Because I'm still starving.

"Do *not* follow me to my office," I tell her sternly.

"Follow you to your office? Get over yourself." Now she's snickering. "Actually, I would do that," she murmurs to herself. "You may need my help in a few minutes."

I take her in again. Take in her dark wavy hair and sharp blue eyes. The dress she's wearing is long, with a bold floral print practically down to the floor. It's belted off, making her waist appear tiny. Large boho hoop earrings I catch a glimpse of when she tosses her head to laugh at me again.

She thinks I'm ridiculous; I can see it in her mocking eyes.

I narrow mine. "What department are you in?"

A brief hesitation. "Marketing."

So she does work here, in one of the creative departments, which makes sense because she comes off as the creative type— you know how some people just have a *look* about them that gives you small clues about who they are?

"What's your name?" The question comes out a bit blunt and slightly rude, but I'm hungry goddammit and haven't eaten breakfast—no bites from the bagel in my hand that's no doubt going to kill me if I ingest it.

"What's yours?" she counters, evading the question with a question of her own.

I relent. "Phillip."

"Hmm." A few sips of her orange juice through pursed yet smiling lips.

"Okay, well." I hold up the napkin, bagel wrapped inside, taking the coffee mug from the counter, pointing toward the door. "Back to work."

"Good luck with that." The young woman points at my snack. "Holler if you need me to hold your hair back when you're on your knees puking in the bathroom."

"Sure. If you say so." I scoff at her one last time before heading back to my office; I've spent far too long dicking around in the breakroom—not that anyone *but Paul* will notice since my supervisor typically works from his vehicle and barely makes appearances.

Twenty steps and I'm almost in the clear, out of view.

Ten more and I can dump this bagel in the trash, scavenge for something that's not going to make me hurl my—

"Did you get the memo?" a voice asks just as I'm passing through the main reception area.

Paul.

He startles me and I almost drop the loosely palmed bagel in my left hand.

Fuckin A, Paul, don't sneak up on a dude like that.

Of course, I don't say that out loud because he'd probably tell someone I was being offensive and get me written up—I might be great at my job, but I have a tendency to be late; the last thing I need is him tallying a list of transgressions. Like: not opening company emails.

I hesitate, stopping in my tracks, still procrastinating. "What memo?"

Paul sighs, inconvenienced, despite the fact that he's the one who stopped me and not the other way around. "They're ripping the carpet out in this side of the building and replacing it."

We literally just spoke—he couldn't have shared this news before?

"Okay." I'm not quite sure what he's getting at. Little slow on the uptake since I am withering away to nothing; I haven't even had breakfast yet. "When?"

"Tomorrow. Which means you won't be able to use your office tomorrow through Friday."

Tomorrow? Through Friday? That's almost the entire work week! "Shouldn't they have given us a heads-up about that?"

"Uh, *hellooo*—I just mentioned the *memo?*"

He doesn't have to sound so snooty. "Yeah, but who actually reads those?"

Paul rolls his eyes, our earlier banter so easily forgotten in light of my brain fart. He sighs again, though I'm convinced he enjoys lording information over me and being in the know. So much for bonding over my dog this morning.

"Janitorial staff are moving desks around overnight and grouping people together so we won't have to work from home."

"What does that mean—grouping people together?" That doesn't sound promising—or private.

"It means you're sharing an office with someone, so play nice."

Play nice? When am I not nice? I might not be up Paul's ass and overly friendly, but I'm not an asshole, either. Mostly.

"Why can't we work from home?" Humphrey would be beside himself to have me home this week. Although…to be fair, he is a ridiculously loud breather and usually doesn't leave me alone when I'm home. He with his large body and ability to squeeze into spots he shouldn't be—like under my feet at the table, and on my lap when I'm trying to do shit on the computer. It's unlikely that I would accomplish anything from home; I've tried in the past and failed.

"The rooms on the north end are large enough to double up on desks, and the execs want everyone to continue working and not slacking off, so HR will email you today with the office you'll be squatting in."

Translation: they don't trust us and are holding us hostage during the renovation.

Great.

Juuust great.

I get to share someone's office space.

Suddenly, my asthmatic, allergy-ridden mutt isn't looking so bad after all. Suddenly, a few days at home with Humphrey don't sound so miserable.

Absentmindedly, because it's in my hand and I'm suddenly tense, I stuff the bagel in my face, biting off a hunk, and chew.

Gag.

Jesus Christ, this thing tastes terrible!

"Trash can," I wheeze through choking sounds, the congealed cream cheese festering on my taste buds and making me want to fucking vomit. "Trash can, now!"

Paul stands abruptly, thrusting the bin into my chest. "Oh my gawd, do *not* puke on my clean marble floors."

He gags a little, sympathy reflex triggered.

I gag.

Paul gags.

I vomit into the garbage, then dry-heave like a pussy, trying to breathe through my nose and failing miserably, the wretched aroma of expired dairy filling the metal bin and my lungs. I toss the bagel in along with the curdled, half-chewed chunk.

Sputter, wanting to scrape my tongue off.

Beside me, Paul continues gagging.

I gag some more.

Raising my eyes, I find the *last* person in the world I wanted to see watching me. Perfect, judgmental brows raised, lips curled. Dark brown hair framing her shrewd, snickering gaze.

I set the garbage can down on the ground next to Paul's desk and rise to my full height, wiping my mouth and puffing out my chest.

"Don't. Say. It."

Her lips part. Close. Part once more to emit a soft, "I told you it would make you throw up."

My nostrils flare, partly because I can't smell anything besides rancid cheese and barf, partly because she insists on vexing me.

"I just asked you not to say anything."

"No, you asked me not to say 'it', presumably 'I told you so.' Which I didn't—not technically."

Why is she still standing here? She needs to walk away.

This is humiliating enough without her as an audience. *Paul is going to hate me after this.*

I stiffen my spine, mortified, turning my back and starting toward the technical side of the office floor, the side where we get our hands dirty and make decisions about concrete and wiring and building codes. Not the fluffy side where they design logos and brochures and signage.

Her side.

Good—I could use the separation. If I had to bump into her

all day, I'd do the unmanliest thing I could think of and curl up and die.

"Aren't you going to wash your hands?" her voice says to my back, taunting me some more. "It's pretty gross."

She will not let this rest.

But she's right—I should totally wash my hands.

"You're gross," Paul repeats, as if I wasn't well aware.

I feel gross, my mouth feels gross, my stomach is in a curdled knot.

"Thanks, man." I check the watch encircling my wrist before making the bathroom my next targeted destination. *Eight forty in the morning and my day has already gone to shit.*

"Um, hellooo," Paul calls to my retreating form. "You can't just leave your puke in my garbage can!"

I need a drink, and there is one way to make this shitty day better: the Bastard Bachelor Society.

2

PHILLIP

Bastard Bachelor Society.

What is it exactly?

It's a gentlemen's club of sorts, like the dignified men of the past used to have—except we're not gentlemen, and we're not dignified. Three ineligible dudes who are bored, jaded, and not looking for relationships. Quite the opposite, actually...

We're so committed to being single, we've created a high-stakes bet to see who can remain single the longest. Rules are involved.

Rule 1: *No member of the society shall date the same person exclusively while an active member of the society.*

Rule 2: *No seeing the same woman more than three nights a week. Mix it up.*

Rule 3: *No giving gifts.*

That's an easy one for me—I'm a cheap son of a bitch who never buys anyone anything, let alone a woman, unless it's my mother. In fact, when I was younger—think college—I broke up with my girlfriends before every Christmas, Valentine's Day, and birthday just to avoid spending money on gifts.

Rule 4: *No marriage or babies.*

Duh.

Rule 5: *We don't speak of the BBS.*

Rule 6: *Never let a girl wear your BBS smoking jacket.*

That's right. We have blue velvet smoking jackets. Don't ask, don't judge. Look away when you see us gathered in our finery and we won't judge you for going to the bar in jeans and a button-down shirt.

Rule 7: *If you want out of the BBS, it has to go to a vote. Same goes for adding new members.*

The whole club was meant as a lark, started by my best friend Brooks Bennett when he was coming off a bad day at the office. Also, his girlfriend had recently broken up with him; it was a breakup he couldn't quite shake. (I know, I know—Brooks is a completely douchey name, but then again, Brooks is a complete and utter douchebag, so it suits him the way red lipstick suits a stripper.)

I've been celibate as a monk for the past few months, so I figured what's the harm in engaging in a little fun? Besides, we each got a sweet club jacket as a reward, compliments of my sister. Brooks had to surrender his the day he confessed to having a girlfriend.

No, that's not what he did—he didn't confess to having a *girlfriend*, he confessed that he'd *fallen in love*. He hadn't even told her about it before he told us, because the weasel was trying to keep his club membership. Wanted us to bend the rules.

As if. Not when there was a bet to win and prizes on the table.

What do we win if we're the last man standing?

Season tickets to the Jags, our local minor league baseball team. A timeshare for a vacation rental. One all-terrain vehicle, which was my contribution. Granted, we all live in the city and I don't know why I own one to begin with, but I intend to keep the dumb thing, along with the rest of the swag.

Those season tickets *will* be mine.

So who is left? Who are the two Bastards still in the game?

Me and Blaine.

Is it childish that we're doing this? Yes.

Does it go against everything our parents taught us about love and relationships? Also yes.

Do we care? *No.*

Did we take pity on our friend Brooks when he fell in love and came crawling to us on his hands and knees, begging us to let him keep his beloved season tickets? The tickets his grandfather left him when he passed away?

Also a big, fat no.

I dial Brooks first; he answers in a hushed tone, greeting me by asking, "Sup."

I add Blaine to the call, and a few seconds later, he dings in, too.

"Hey."

Sup. Hey. Bunch of cunning linguists we are.

I grunt, not wasting time with idle chitchat since there's no telling when someone will have to hang up, considering we're all at work.

"I blew chunks in the waste paper basket at work."

There's a silence. A long, exaggerated pause before Blaine asks, "What's a waste paper basket?"

"Jesus H," Brooks mutters. "It's a damn garbage can." I hear him take a bite of something then spit the remnants into the trash, most likely a pistachio shell because those are his favorite. He chews thoughtfully. "Why'd you barf?"

"I ate expired cream cheese."

Murmurs of understanding all around; eating expired food is a guy thing—one they both understand.

"What's the big deal?"

"A girl in my office saw me."

Another pause. "*And?*"

"She's going to lord it over me."

"So what, big deal, she saw you heave in the trash," Blaine says nonchalantly, and I hear his keyboard clicking in the background. "Do you have a crush on her?"

No.

"Wait." Brooks halts the conversation. "Is this the girl from the accounting department who watches you over the wall of her cubicle?"

"No." *Thank God.*

Brooks lets out a *hmm.* "Is it the chick from sales who walks by your office four times a day pretending to be looking for your boss?"

Yeah, she's weird, too. "No, it's not that woman." I pause, not sure how much of my day I should share, then inhale. "There's more to this story."

"There's more than a woman at work watching you toss your cookies?"

"Yes," I groan, watching through the window of my office to make sure no one is walking by—my door is open and the last thing I need is one of my colleagues overhearing me gossiping about myself. "I barfed in the trash can...of the guy who answers the phones...and then...he started gagging, too."

The line is silent.

"Kind of like a pity gag?" Blaine's question is cautious, as if he's weighing his words.

"Yeah." I stare up at the ceiling. "*Exactly* like a pity gag."

More silence—which is so unlike my friends. They love nothing more than to mock me and make fun of the stupid things I do, and puking at work—in front of other people—is as good as it gets if you're looking for roasting material.

They take pity on me. Sort of.

"Hold up." Blaine laughs. "Are you telling us that not only did this chick see you puke, she watched as the other dude was gagging, too?"

"That's exactly what I'm saying." Haven't they been paying attention?

"Is she good-looking?"

My long hesitation is the only confirmation these two dipshits need.

"Yeah, she's never going to let you live that down."

One of them bites into something, swallows. "It's a good thing you can't date anyone, because that's one woman who isn't going to want anything to do with your stinky, gag-inducing ass."

"Gee, thanks."

Brooks' implied shrug echoes through the phone. "Just calling it like I see it."

"No offense," Blaine adds, "but no chick from your office is ever going to date you now with barf breath, and unfortunately, you haven't gone out enough lately to meet any other women. Zero dates."

"Ha ha." Not funny. I know plenty of women, and *hello*—who even meets people in real life anymore? That's what dating apps are for, duh. "I never said I wanted to date anyone from the office."

They don't believe me, and I wonder why the hell I called them in the first place. Rookie mistake.

"Bet she could write up a fun little slogan about the puker in office B." Brooks laughs uproariously, pouncing on the idea.

"Oh, you're a comedian now?"

"Stating facts, that's all. If I were her, I'd report you in the company newsletter." Brooks thinks he's so goddamn clever.

"You have a company newsletter?" Blaine asks. "We don't."

"We have a company handbook," I tell them.

"What does it say about fraternizing? Not that it matters because no one there wants to date you."

"Once again—thank you for pointing out the obvious."

"Hey, that's what we're here for." Blaine is chuckling at his lame jokes. "We're also here to help you lose the bet, so date away. Let her fall in love with you. Lay on the charm—oh wait, you already laid it in the garbage can in the form of ralphing."

Brooks cuts in. "Speaking of losing the bet, what I want to know is…is this girl cute? The one who saw you blow chunks."

I ignore that last part of his sentence, shrugging even though they can't see me. "I guess so."

"He guesses so." Brooks laughs into the phone. "Uh-oh, boys, we know what that means. Another one bites the dust."

"What did I say? What?" I sound defensive, even to my own ears. "I said *I guess so*—that's it. I didn't call her hot or smokin' or pretty. I said I guess she's cute. Big freaking deal."

"As Shakespeare once said, thou doesn't protesteth too much, my lady," Blaine scoffs.

"Uh, first of all, it's 'Thou doth protest too much, methinks.' And second of all, I don't have time to argue with either of you. I'm not going to lose the bet."

I'm going to win it.

"You idiots both fucked up the quote," Brooks interjects bossily. "It's 'The lady doth protest too much, methinks.' Jesus Christ, get it together. Don't you know anything?"

Blaine sighs. "What's this mystery girl's name?"

"I don't know."

"What do you mean you *don't know*?"

I feel my face getting red. "She wouldn't tell me."

Blaine cackles. "What. A. Ballbuster!"

"Is that what we're calling it now when a girl is rude and sarcastic? A ballbuster?" I'm getting irritated now, even more so than before. "And do you want to know what else? This is her fault. She told me not to eat the cream cheese but then watched me eat it, *then* watched me throw up in the waste paper basket."

"That's a you problem, not a her problem," Blaine murmurs. "And please stop using the term waste paper basket—you sound like my grandmother. It's weird."

"Do you know how you sound right now, Phillip? You sound like a kid in the back seat of his parents' minivan, whining to his mom because his sister is looking at him."

"Well she *was* looking at me." And I didn't like it.

"You problem," he says again.

"Stop it," I whine, well aware that it sounds like I'm pouting.

But shit, I'm taking a beating today. First from Paul, then from the bagel that wrecked my insides, now from my friends—who are supposed to be on my side.

Traitors.

Why are they so goddamn infuriating? "My point is, I'm irritated."

"Because of a girl."

Yes, one hundred percent. "No, because I puked at work."

"In front of a girl," they both say at the same time.

I let out a *pfft* and shift in my desk chair. The chair I have to eventually evacuate today, inside the office I have to clean out so workers can come in and tear out the flooring tomorrow. "It doesn't matter—I've never bumped into her before today and I doubt I ever will again."

"Famous. Last. Words." Brooks' taunt makes my lip snarl up.

"Why did I bother calling the two of you? I called so you could cheer me up, not make me feel like a pile of shit."

"Do you need us to bring you some soup and rub your tummy?" Blaine can barely contain his laughter as the barbs continue rolling. "I might have some saltine crackers in my desk."

"Shut up, asshole."

Only—he's not really being an asshole, because I know damn well he would bring me soup and crackers and whatever else I needed. Blaine Shepard might be a douchebag sometimes, but he's a great friend.

All I'd need to do is ask and he'd be here.

I've known these jackasses since we were in high school; we parted ways in college, each taking our own individual paths, attending different universities. Somehow, though, we all ended up in Chicago. Close enough to downtown that we can meet a few times a month—or week—for drinks, cigars, and trash talk. Talk about work. Our families. Love lives.

Lack thereof…

Women.

And now, with the inception of the Bastard Bachelor Society —or the BBS, as we've begun calling it—we have more reason to get together than we did before.

"Seriously though, dude. If you need anything..." Brooks laments thoughtfully, his tone changing, more serious. I can hear the clicking of a pen in the background, imagining his thumb pressing down on it over and over and over while we talk, to keep his hands occupied.

Suddenly, I feel better. Not so butthurt. "I'll be fine. I'm not actually sick."

"But you could get food poisoning, dipshit. You should go get checked out."

"I'm not going to the doctor, *Mom*. I won't get food poisoning." And I can't afford to get it, either. The last thing I want is to visit the doctor, ain't no one got time, even if it comes with a free prostate exam. "I'll be fine."

Blaine isn't convinced. "If you say so." Then, "Should we have a meeting this week or skip it until you're your old self again?"

There is a silence on the line as they wait for my verdict. "Let's have a meeting." I need one.

I'm being kicked out of my own office all week.

I need to vent, and I need a drink.

3

SPENCER

Tuesday morning and already they've managed to squeeze another desk inside my office.

Clearly an act of God, this new interloper has managed to be crushed in—by what forces I may never know since I wasn't here when they brought the desk in—all the unnecessary furniture temporarily removed and stacked outside my door.

Two chairs and a plant stand. One thin, three-tiered book shelf.

Whose stupid idea was this? Why not just leave the desks out in the common areas?

Deciding a man must have made this decision—no offense to any men out there, but *come on now*—I narrow my eyes, assessing the situation with palpable irritation. Coming face-to-face with a mega-desk is not how I wanted to begin my Tuesday morning.

Or any morning for that matter.

Still.

Dubbing it the mega-desk will at least be amusing for me, since that's what it looks like. A monolith of wood taking up space I simply do not have in this office.

An office I do not want to share.

Call me selfish, or territorial, but...

I don't.

Regardless, I have no choice.

I stare at the two desks, scooting my way around them, into the cramped space, moving the door to see whether it can be shut or not. I may be giving up privacy for the next few days, but it would be nice to have a closed door considering we'll have twice as many people on this side of the floor during the renovations.

I test it, giving a definitive nod when the door barely misses the extra desk, then continue toward my chair.

Of course, this new arrangement also means this week I'll have an officemate from the opposite end of the building—the south side. The *construction* side. A person—probably a man—I pray will not chatter, will not distract me during the days they're invading my space.

And it *is* mine.

Mine, mine, mine.

I relish it. I busted my ass for it. *I loves it.*

Mine.

Dumping my purse on the marble windowsill, I pull my chair out and survey the landscape with my hands on my hips; it's a gorgeous day. The sun is shining through the windows, and though it's cold, there are birds in the trees. The bright beams hit my computer screen in such a way that I can see it's been wiped clean by cleaning staff.

Keyboard, too.

I power everything up with a content hum in my throat and a pep in my step. Plug in my phone charger. Shuffle and rearrange my pens and highlighters, busying myself with mundane tasks while I wait.

I wonder who my roomie is going to be, what department they're in. The memo only stated that "*the south side of the complex will be getting new carpeting first, then when that is complete, the north side will get an overhaul. Please excuse our mess during the renovation.*"

I had to visit the company website for a map to see which departments were on the south side of this expansive floor—male-dominated departments like equipment, development, estimating, and contracts. The project managers and superintendents have offices on that side of the floor, too.

Why am I fidgeting? This is my office—I'm not the gatecrasher who has to squat in someone else's space for the week.

Granted, it's not my choice, but still—show some respect!

I sigh, sweeping the hair out of my eyes, glancing out the window at the street below. Listen to the sounds of traffic and the train and the honking—noise pollution I used to hate with a passion but have grown to love.

A city girl at heart, I always knew I would stay here. Born and bred with a subway card in her back pocket and a chip on her shoulder where tourists are concerned, it seems fitting I would end up working in an industry where, as a female, I have to hold my own. Have to stiffen my spine and stand my ground when I believe in something strongly.

I watch the sidewalk as pedestrians come and go, heads bent, hurried. On their way to work, or to grab coffee, or take their kids to school. Late for the subway, late for a meeting, early. On time. People, people, everywhere.

Speaking of coffee, I wish I had some now.

I didn't want to trickle in this morning, assuming I would find someone in the other desk when I arrived. There's nothing I love more than playing hostess in my apartment—it's another thing entirely to be sharing my office. Even so, I was up bright and early, showered and out the door an entire hour ahead of schedule.

So unlike me.

I did, however, draw the line at grabbing breakfast for the new half of this temporary duo—God forbid I make them feel *too* welcome or *too* comfortable. Get them in and get them out; that will be my motto for the duration of the week.

The clock ticks.

Car horns blare.

The train car on the next block screeches on its rusted rails.

Tick.

Tock.

"Well. I suppose I could get some work done," I say to no one in particular, giving my wireless speaker a longing look. I love listening while I work, preferring talk radio or stand-up comedy to get the creative juices flowing. Would it be rude to have the speaker playing when this person *finally* arrives?

Tick.

Tock.

I quite literally twiddle my thumbs. Move the mouse for my computer around to pass the time when I should be working. Instead, I'm hemming and hawing waiting on this person. This stranger. Let's face it—I don't socialize with the construction side much, so the chances that I'm going to be familiar with my officemate? Slim to none.

I stare out the window. Putz around on social media.

I have an ad campaign to busy myself with, but I don't touch it. There's signage for a huge high-rise to finalize, colors for a new exterior to look at and who has time to screw around?! Not me!

"Ugh." I heave myself out of the desk chair, irritated and impatient, stomach fluttering like it did my freshman year of college waiting on my first ever roommate. *Will she want the bed I chose? Will she be a total bitch? Will she be tidy like I am or a complete slob like my sister Shannon?*

Tick.

Tock.

It's just past eight o'clock in the morning. Around here, the workday has officially begun for almost everyone in our building, and my cellmate has yet to arrive.

My stomach growls, and because I skipped breakfast to make a hasty trip to work this morning, I resign myself to the breakroom, where I know there's at least a muffin or bagel or two.

I snicker, remembering yesterday—Phillip.

Phillip, the guy who loaded up his bagel with expired cream cheese to be stubborn and prove a point, then barfed it back up in the garbage can in reception. He might have been cute in his standard-issue company polo and jeans—but the sounds he made when he gagged?

Disgusting, and also hilarious.

I bet when he gets the sniffles, he's useless for days.

A "man cold" my mother calls it when my dad gets sick. One sniffle, one cough or slight fever and my father is laid out flat, bellyaching on the bed as if dying of some incurable plague —like a child.

Drives my mom *nuts*.

My mind strays to the image of him, hunched over and vomiting in Paul's trash, and Paul beside him, eyes wide, hand on his mouth as if he were about to wretch, too.

There was no time for me to mention that one time in fifth grade during English class, we were seated on the floor listening to our teacher, Mrs. Galvin, when suddenly, I threw up in Renee Hall's lap. When we were sent to the bathroom to clean ourselves up—me apologizing profusely—Renee threw up in the sink.

So yeaaaah.

Definitely not worth mentioning my own humiliation, instead enjoying Phillip's.

The look on that guy's face...classic mortification when his horrified gaze met mine from across the lobby. I was the last person he wanted to witness him puking.

Honestly? I kind of feel terrible for him.

Okay fine, on a scale of one to ten, I feel terrible negative zero, because witnessing that moment was a gift from above—

ammunition for a rainy day, in case I ever bump into him, or need a favor.

Shoot, come to think of it, why didn't I film it with my phone to use as evidence?

In any case, I am absolutely not going to the breakroom because I'm hoping to bump into Phillip. Who I absolutely *do not* have a crush on in any way, shape, or form. I just met the guy, for heaven's sake—no one develops a crush that fast, no matter how ruggedly handsome someone is. Or how amazing he smells. *Especially* after watching that someone vomit in the most ungentlemanly fashion.

I'm hungry and need coffee; that's my reason for heading to the breakroom. Taking the long route through accounting, past receivables, along the corridor past purchasing, the department that awards subcontractor contracts.

Glass walls. Easily visible offices. Fish bowls.

Except today, they're all empty, void of even furniture.

Eventually I arrive at my destination, peeking into the empty room with hesitation—large, full of windows, all the amenities you'd find in the kitchen at your house and then some. Refrigerator. Sink. Several sets of tables and chairs. A few booths along the wall. Cabinets with plates, bowls, and glasses. Drawers with cutlery.

But no Phillip.

I'm not disappointed—*you* are.

I mosey on in, ambling to the fridge. A few times a week, food is brought in, not by our budget-conscience company, but by other businesses wanting jobs with us. Flooring contractors send in bagels on Fridays. The glass and window manufacturer? Monthly barbeque. There's the occasional taco bar—hence why I've literally gained ten pounds since I began working here.

My eyes linger on the door.

No Phillip.

Since it's Tuesday, there are croissants on the counter, and I snatch one from the glass bell jar, wrap it in a napkin, and pop it in the microwave for twenty seconds.

Not very nutritious, but buttery and delicious.

I'm cramming the baked good into my mouth when he strolls in, real classy and casual. A hot flush floods my cheeks.

Crap.

I may have seen him toss his cookies yesterday, but I did not need him to see *me* stuffing my face. Not a good look for me.

"Morning." Phillip sidles over, reaching for a coffee mug, laptop bag slung over his shoulder. His hair is still wet and he smells like fresh shower, shampoo, and aftershave lotion—all the best things combined.

He's wearing a black sweater and jeans, and when he turns his back to fill his cup, I can't stop my eyes from roaming his broad back.

Dog hair.

Dog hair everywhere.

Yikes.

I stifle a laugh, wondering what kind of hound he has that sheds so bad, and feel guilty all over again for this poor dude's bad luck.

"Feeling better today?" I jab, unable to stop myself.

"Yes," he grunts. Turns. Spears me with a blue-eyed stare. "I wasn't sick."

We both know he wasn't sick, but that doesn't stop me from raising my perfect brows into my hairline and taunting, "You weren't? Weird. Usually when someone heaves, it's because they're not feeling well." For my next bite of warm croissant, I delicately pull the other end up and set it on my waiting tongue. "Just saying."

"I feel fine."

He looks fine. Super fine and super cute.

Ugh. I wish he'd go away so I could scarf down the remainder of this bread, but he doesn't. In the brief time he's been standing in the breakroom, he has only poured himself a mug of steaming coffee, hasn't taken a single sip, nor has he gotten anything to eat.

I go to the fridge, pull the door open. Retrieve the white, round container of cream cheese and extend it as an offering. "Here."

When he doesn't take it, I set it on the counter between us. Poke it with my finger to give it a nudge in his direction. When he doesn't touch it, I remove the lid, smiling. Am I the absolute worst or what?

Phillip gags, a small choking sound in the back of his throat.

What a pussy. Seriously.

"I'm not..." He turns his back for a few seconds, inhaling the fresh air. "I'm not hungry." When he faces me again, he practically wheezes, eyes narrowed in my direction, and I shrug, heading toward the door.

"You should toss that—it might make someone sick," I say over my shoulder. "Then again, who'd be dumb enough to eat it?"

Grabbing a water bottle from the cabinet next to the exit, I make my way through the wide corridor with the smirk still on my face.

But. Someone is behind me.

I glance back.

Correction: *Phillip* is behind me.

I turn right, toward the creative department.

Phillip turns right toward the creative department, hoisting his laptop bag, redistributing the weight.

I halt in my tracks, spinning on my heels. "Are you following me?"

"It does appear that way."

Hmm. "Where are you headed?"

He lifts his arm, pointing down the hallway, then moves past, squeezing between me and the wall because, well—I'm just standing here blocking his path. Not on purpose, I just...would rather stand here talking stupid and flirting than relegate myself to the confines of the mega-desk awaiting me.

Sigh.

I watch Phillip's strong back, muscles straining through the knit of his sweater, dog hair clinging, yet oddly enough it's not bothering me to see it there.

He hangs a left.

I hang a left.

Phillip halts in his tracks, turning. "Are *you* following *me?*"

Gross. "No!" Technically, I am, though not on purpose. "Where are you going?"

"Temporary housing." He has a small piece of paper in his hand I hadn't noticed before, most likely an office number.

Ah. Definitely from the south side of the building.

Interesting.

Phillip checks each doorplate, glancing at the numbered offices as he strolls by. Hangs another left in the labyrinthine maze that is the thirtieth story.

I'm still behind him, feeling quite like a stalker, slowly trailing along, half-eaten croissant and water bottle in hand, staring at the back of his head. Dark, short, wet hair, a bit longer on top. Expansive shoulders. Strong upper arms. Phillip is tall and rugged, unlike so many of the men in this city. Metrosexuals aren't my type, so I've practically given up dating. A man who takes longer than I do to get ready on a Saturday night? Intolerable.

Phillip slows, nodding politely at Monica in graphic design as she impolitely gawks through the glass windows of her design space, a spare desk crammed against hers.

Someone must have started a group chat, because several younger women rise from their cubicles like prairie dogs and peep their heads over the short walls to watch Phillip amble by. I hear their subtle murmuring, the low-key whispers. *Who is that? Oh my God, he is so cute. Please let him come to my office, please let him come to my office…*

Ladies, get it together, says the look I shoot them from behind my wall of glass. They're embarrassing the creative department!

Phillip stops, framed in the doorway to my office. Checks the sheet of paper against the number posted next to my door. Takes one step toward the mega-desk, then another, then—

No.

No, no, no.

He cannot be my officemate for the rest of the week. Cannot. I won't stand for it! How am I supposed to live like this, holed up with this cutie of a guy who smells like mountains, and who I wouldn't mind giving up my single-lady status for?

I groan when he walks all the way inside, shrugging the laptop bag off his shoulder, dumping it onto his desk chair—as if he's done it a million times before.

I stand in the threshold, clutching the croissant to my chest. Stare, slack-jawed.

"You have *got* to be kidding me."

He glances over at me as if he'd forgotten I was behind him, already unzipping his bag. "Please don't say this is your office."

Chin up, Spencer. Chin. Up.

I tilt it jauntily, summoning some false bravado, and waltz past him to plop down in my chair. Heft my legs and prop them up, entwining my fingers behind my head as if I own the place. "Okay, I won't say it."

My officemate is the puker.

The puker is my officemate.

Phillip stands frozen at his desk but makes no move to sit his butt down; he's stiff and rigid and miserable.

I gesture toward his chair like we're starting a meeting. "Please, do have a seat."

I swear, he narrows his eyes at me, an insult no doubt on the tip of his tongue. He bites it. "I *will*, but not because you told me to."

"Please." I make a show of fanning my arms out theatrically. "Be my guest."

Phillip's nostrils flare, but he does not sit. "Got it. Thanks."

"Like—any day now."

Now there is no mistaking the blue eyes sliding into slits in my direction. "Let's get a few things straight."

"A few things straight?" I lift my eyebrows. Purse my lips. Make a show of shuffling some printer paper; it's blank, primarily used for doodling, sometimes for printing—neither are things I plan on doing right now. "I can't wait to hear this."

"We just have to make it through the next four days. Can you not..." His voice trails off as he chooses his words, hand moving airily about. "The farce isn't necessary."

"What farce?"

"You don't have to pretend to be nice. I know you're not."

"I am nice!" I gasp, insulted. "Why would you say that?"

He ignores me. "Furthermore, we should lay down a few ground rules before you get too comfortable."

"I'm not the one who has to worry about getting too comfortable—you've already worn out your welcome, pal." I emit an unladylike snort. "You're the one squatting in my office, or need I keep reminding you? By all means, lay down some *ground* rules. Just what we need." I urge him on with a wave of my hand. "Go. Please proceed."

It's obvious he's already exasperated by this conversation based on the slouch of his shoulders. "I'd prefer to keep the door open while I'm here, if you don't mind. I don't want anyone thinking anything inappropriate is going on."

Like that *would happen.*

I mean...it could. But it won't.

But it could.

Ugh, why is he so attractive yet annoying?!

"You wanna keep the door open? Fine, but you're going to regret that when Karen from sales sticks her nose in here twelve times a day." I honestly wonder how she hasn't been fired for rarely working, but that's HR's problem, not mine. Karen is a delight, and I welcome the intrusion.

"At least she won't get the wrong idea."

"Wrong idea about what, exactly? That we're working at work, in an office where we work? It's not like I invited you here."

I swear his face gets red. "You *know* what I mean."

Yes, I *know* what he means—but I'm supremely aggravated by the fact Phillip is so full of himself. Does he honestly think I'm not capable of keeping my hands to myself while he's using my office? That he's so irresistible and good-looking I'm going to hit on him all damn day?

If anything, I should be the one paranoid about him! Men can be pigs sometimes, and I do not know this guy from Adam. He's a complete stranger. For all I know, he's a total pervert and I'm stuck with him for almost an entire week.

It's not like management gave us a choice; we all do what we have to do to be team players, so I'm not about to complain to my boss.

I have a large office, thus I was automatically selected to play hostess to whomever was booted from their space so their carpet could be replaced.

Okay fine—it's not *that* large and impressive, especially not with these two desks rammed inside.

"We'll keep the door open, Your Highness, but don't say I didn't warn you." Karen likes to chatter, strolling by on a regular basis throughout the day with news or gossip or donuts. Stick a hot guy inside my space? I plan to see Karen wearing a path in the carpet from her door to mine just to flirt with Phillip.

Good-looking, conceited Phillip.

"Also," he goes on, "I'd prefer not to make small talk. I have work to do and am on deadlines, so..." He avoids my incredulous gaze as he starts unpacking his laptop bag, removing the computer, a few pens, and a calculator.

He's the only one with deadlines? Pompous jerk.

"Just so we're clear—I have nothing to say to you." Unless it's to give the jackass a piece of my mind. "And since we're sharing rules, I want to put it out there…I don't expect you to get me coffee unless you're getting some for yourself."

Phillip's spine stiffens. "Excuse me?"

"I said, I don't expect you to get me coffee unless you're getting some for yourself."

His hands go up to stop me from continuing to speak. "No, no. I heard what you said, I just…won't be getting you coffee. Ever. I'm not your secretary, and this isn't *Working Girl*. I won't be making you copies, or sending emails for you, or doing you favors. Entendido?"

"Is that Spanish?"

"Yes."

I roll my eyes. "Yes, I understand." Pause for dramatic effect, because he's being a drama llama, then add, "Friends get their friends coffee."

"We're not friends. I don't even know your name."

"It's Spencer, and I like traveling to exotic locations, indie films, indie books, and iced lattes with extra ice—would it kill you to grab one for me on your way in every now and again?"

So rude.

"It might."

I give him the heaviest eye roll I can muster. "Drama, drama, drama."

"I'm not getting you snacks, food, or any kind of caffeinated beverage."

I shrug. "Suit yourself."

Phillip gets comfortable at his desk, cracking his knuckles (shudder), flipping his laptop open, and waiting for it to power up. Types in his password. Clicks away at his keyboard with obnoxious, robust taps that will probably drive me nuts within the hour. No—the next minute.

Click.

Click. Click, click, clickety click click click.

Click. Backspace, backspace.

Oh my God!

What could he possibly be working on?! He's been in here less than six minutes! I prefer to ease into my work, warming up by hitting the breakroom, checking my social media, texting my mom and a few friends first. Maybe I'll take a lap around the building to get the creative juices flowing—take advantage of the walk to clear my head, chat with a few people along the way—but I never, *ever* just get straight to work.

Who does that?!

I watch Phillip while using my laptop as cover, its black screen concealing me while I ogle his work ethic incredulously. *What is wrong with this guy? Just look at him, working—making us all look bad!*

"Stop watching me," he tells me without looking up, tapping away like a maniac.

"I'm not."

He looks up. "Stop."

"You're not the boss of me."

"You're not the boss of *me*," he parrots.

"So stop being so bossy." *And stop working—it's not even eight thirty in the morning*, I want to say. *You're making me look bad.*

"If you would just stop staring at me while I'm trying to work, we wouldn't be arguing."

Excuse me if I've never seen anyone on this side of the building get straight to work when they sit down. Sheesh.

"If you weren't working then I wouldn't be staring." Shit. Did I say that part out loud?

"Huh?" Phillip looks so confused.

"Nothing. I meant—don't flatter yourself. I'm not even remotely interested in what you have going on or why you're typing a thousand words a second." I huff.

His head tilts down, eyes engrossed, plastered to his screen. "You seem like the kind of girl who likes to argue." He sighs without having the decency to raise his head, those long fingers rhythmically beating at his keyboard.

The kind of girl who likes to argue! How dare he be so accurate. How. Dare. He.

"You don't know anything about me." I sniff indignantly. "I'm as docile as a house cat." *One that likes to argue.*

I hold back a meow for effect, knowing he'll think it's weird. He's wearing a cable-knit sweater, for pity's sake—and he hasn't smiled at me once.

I don't even know if he has a full set of teeth inside his perfect mouth.

"Docile as a cat?" Phillip snorts. "I know plenty of house cats, all of which would eat your dead body if you collapsed on the floor."

Dang, that's probably true. "I, uh, can't help but noticing you have a pet." There. I've successfully changed the subject. "What kind is it?"

My new officemate *finally* looks up at me, blue eyes quizzical. "How do you know I have a pet?"

"You have hair all over the back of your sweater," I kindly point out. How does he not know this? Is he blind? It wouldn't take a detective long to discover his information.

He curses, letting out a groan, then twists his body in a failed effort to see the back of his black garment. "Do I? Shit, I do."

"Cat or dog?"

"Dog."

"What kind?"

Phillip levels me with a blank stare. "Did we or did we not agree not to make small talk?"

"I agreed to nothing. Are you always this bullheaded? What's the harm in chatting before we get to work?"

The loud sigh he emits causes a few heads in the cubicle area to turn, and I catch Francine Pepperman raising her eyebrows over her partition, because the nosey, eavesdropping woman cannot keep to her own business.

I shrug at her through the glass and she lowers herself back down into her seat.

"It's a dog, his name is Humphrey, he's a Basset Hound, and three out of five days I'm late to work because he cannot get his act together."

He fires off answers before I can ask specifics, describing his dog as if it were a child who won't put his shoes on for school in the morning despite being instructed to do so fifteen times.

"You should leave the house sooner." An icy glare is his only reply, so I add, "Take him out to pee earlier."

Silence.

"Is he the kind of dog that's impossible to wake up?"

Another beleaguered sigh. "I'm going to file a complaint with human resources about your incessant line of questioning."

"This is *my* office."

He hesitates as if not quite sure how to respond but pulls through with a respectable, "I am your *guest*—as you so eloquently pointed out."

"Ah, and therefore, I am trying to make you feel at home by trying to get to know you better."

"No—you're just freaking nosey."

True. He has me there; I am nosey, mostly out of boredom. I don't know if anyone knows this, but creatively marketing for a construction company isn't exactly the most thrilling line of work on the planet. I'm basically designing signs to hang on the side of skyscrapers and postcards to hand out to the community when a large job is about to start, apologizing for the inconvenience. *Please excuse our mess!* kind of thing, the same message we received via memo from management about the remodeling.

I tap a pencil on the surface of my desk, thinking. "It's not a crime to ask questions. You're covered in dog hair—sue me for not wanting you to walk around looking like a human lint roller." I pull open a desk drawer and retrieve a roll of duct tape, sliding it across the surface of the mega-desk. "Here, I don't have a lint roller, but this will do the trick. Just use the sticky side to pull off the hair."

Phillip pushes the tape back with the flat plane of his hand. "You're funny, ha ha."

I know I am. Duh. "I'll bring you one tomorrow. I think I have one lying around in a closet somewhere."

"Please don't."

I put a palm up. "No thanks necessary." I throw in a wink for good measure before pulling my top drawer open and rooting around for earbuds—if he's going to sit and talk, I'll have to drown out his noise. *They must be here somewhere...*

He stops ignoring me. "Are you putting in headphones?"

I point to my ears, which now have buds nestled inside them, cord plugged into the side of my desktop. "What? I can't hear you."

"Are you serious?"

I smirk at him. "Sorry, but you're actually a bit too talkative and I have work to do."

Phillip looks stunned, then pissed, then—he smacks his hands down on the desk, affronted. "I'm the one who told you to be quiet!" he practically shouts.

"Shh." I hold a finger to my lips. "The door has to remain open. Don't want everyone to hear you."

"Oh my God," he mumbles, and I *can* hear him, because I don't actually have any music on. "I'm so over this week already."

4

PHILLIP

D ay. From.
Hell.
That's what this was.

Let me count all the ways things went wrong after I got settled into Her Majesty's office today:

1. She started calling me Puker after I tossed a wadded-up piece of paper into the trash, stating that all garbage cans remind her of me and how I tossed my cookies.
2. When I came back from lunch, there was a small container of fresh cream cheese on my desk chair. Ha ha, *not* funny.
3. Spencer Standish hums when she's sketching storyboards.
4. Spencer Standish hums when she's using the computer.
5. Spencer Standish hums. Period. Not cute little songs or tunes a person would recognize—no. Her hum is more of an unquiet, out-of-tune palindrome. If she

were humming outside, dogs would howl and cats
would growl, i.e., terrible. Tone deaf. Dreadful
humming.

6. She licked her fingers after eating an orange. Sixteen
times. I would know, because I counted. One lick
after each bite, then she cleaned her digits one by
one when she was done. Use a damn napkin next
time!

7. Spencer would not share her orange, and I didn't
even know I wanted a slice until I smelled its citrusy
goodness wafting over and promptly wanted some.
She refused—so not hospitable of her.

Body tired, brain exhausted, I hip-bump the front door of
my brownstone open, toss my keys down, shrug off my jacket,
and squat, knowing that in five...four...three...two...

One.

Humphrey lumbers gaily around the corner, swiftly as a
Basset Hound can, encumbered by long ears, a long body, and
an overweight midsection. He howls enthusiastically, belting out
a low bleat, on guard for the moment it takes him to realize I am
not an intruder infiltrating the castle he must defend, bleary-
eyed and fresh from his afternoon snooze.

Humphrey finishes bellowing when he realizes it's me, tail
wagging, hard and hitting the coffee table, magazines sliding
from its surface with every bang, onto the hardwood floor.

One more thing for me to clean up.

"Hey boy! Hey!" I scratch behind his ears. "Did you
miss me?"

Wet dog nose drifts to my pockets, sniffing for a treat. Surely
there is one for him inside!

Sadly, there is not.

"Not today, boy. I'm fresh out, but I promise I'll have some
for you tomorrow." I give him a few more pats on the top of his
soft, smooth head. "Wanna go for a walk?"

His tail thumps harder. Yes.

"Let me take a piss and we'll go. Get your leash!" I tell him, pointing to the mudroom where it hangs. "Go get your leash!"

Humphrey does *not* get his leash.

Lazy bastard.

I stand, walking past him to the bathroom, and shut the door; if I don't lock him out, his nose will be all up in my business, sniffing while I try to pee. Like a toddler who insists on being in the toilet with its mother, his body would take up half the space in the tiny room and make the simple act of peeing much more difficult.

Turning my back so it's facing the mirror, I crane my neck to glance over my shoulder at the back of my sweater. Sure as shit, it's covered in Humphrey hair, auburn against black and stuck straight out like porcupine needles in a few spots.

Great. *Just great*—this can't be the first time I've walked out of the house with a body full of dog hair, and I don't own a single goddamn lint brush.

I wonder for a split second if Spencer will actually bring me one tomorrow, like she said she would, then shrug off the idea—why the hell am I thinking about her at all? Let alone wondering if she's going to bring me gifts.

A lint brush is not a gift, you tool.

In short order, I have the dog on his lead—a bright blue leash with small, red fire hydrants on it, though Humphrey has never peed on a fire hydrant a day in his life—and we're out the door, briskly making our way down the sidewalk.

Instantly, Humphrey has his nose to the ground, the relentless sniffing so loud I can hear it a few feet away, his long body hard at work.

Walk, *sniff*, walk, *sniff*.

Pause.

Sniff.

I let him do his thing—he never gets straight to the deed in the afternoons (the way Spencer didn't get straight to work this morning), not after being cooped up in the house the entire day, so I give him the freedom to poke around.

Goofy little dude deserves it.

I got him as a rescue when he was eight months old; he was a monster as a puppy, and his owners surrendered him. I couldn't imagine why when I first saw him—he was fucking adorable with his doe eyes, and droopy mouth, and giant ears. How could anything that cute be such a holy terror?

Well. I found out soon enough—came home one afternoon after making the mistake of letting Puppy Humphrey roam the house while I ran to the grocery store and found that the devil had destroyed the living room. Tore up a pillow. Ripped a sofa cushion. And how had shorty gotten up onto the coffee table? How had he ripped up the mail that'd been sitting on the counter?

Luckily for me, as he grew, he stopped ruining shit.

Unfortunately for me, Humphrey is a taker, and he takes advantage of the leeway now, maneuvering his trunk-like body into a line of shrubs.

It's not an easy task—Humphrey hasn't missed a meal in years—but he manages, disappearing entirely until the only body part I can see is his tail. He pulls at the leash, determined to drag me into the shrubs, too, but I stand firm on the sidewalk, arms crossed until he finishes doing whatever he's doing.

Sniffing. Digging. Snooping.

It's in his blood, I have to remind myself. *Be patient; it's in his blood.* A detective he will never be, but damned if he doesn't try.

I stand by the street, holding his leash steady while he does his doggy thang, and find myself staring off into space…fixating on the bricks of the neighboring building, brain taking me back to that place.

Back.

To.

Spencer.

God. If I have anything to say about spending the workday with her, if I had to choose one word to describe it, that word would be *infuriating*.

But.

If I'm being honest, I didn't exactly hate it. I put on a good front, protesting every time she decided to play music to fill the quiet room. Acted like the donuts she went back and stole from the breakroom were disgusting and possibly poisoned—but when she wasn't looking, I snatched one and scarfed it down the way Humphrey scarfs down the rare human table scrap.

Goddamn that donut tasted good.

Maybe officing with a female won't be the worst, although Spencer could make it easier by toning down the obnoxious meter. By not humming.

I flick Humphrey's leash as a five-minute warning, dreading the moment that dog walks out of the bushes with a face full of mud (like he did the last time I let him dally). He's done it a million times, and if he does it tonight, I'm going to be pissed. No one has time to give him a bath this close to bedtime. No one.

After his time is up, I flick the leash again, emitting a few clicks of my tongue. "Come on, boy. Playtime is over, time to get serious."

For a brief second, I think he's going to ignore me—like he usually does—then the little dude astonishes me when he listens, backing out of the shrubs like a mini dump truck. Beep, beep, beep!

His rear wiggles, tail wagging, as usual.

We both smile.

Happy dog, happy life.

5

SPENCER

Captain's log: Wednesday.

I may or may not have taken special care with my appearance this morning. Longer time with my makeup, more time choosing my outfit, special care with my hair—none of which has absolutely anything to do with a certain good-looking, male officemate.

None at all.

Er.

Maybe a little.

Possibly?

I'm at the office early again today (for the second day in a row), having practically flown here on wings built of sheer excitement. The lint brush I set on the seat of his desk chair is like the lone present you're impatient for your parents to open on Christmas Day.

Except they dawdle and make coffee first.

Phillip still is not here.

I twiddle my thumbs again, quite literally, fiddling and fidgeting as if I were in high school again, waiting for my crush to show up for math class.

Slowly, time passes. Eight o'clock.

Nine o'clock.

Nine fifteen.

Nine thirty-two.

Maybe he isn't coming back. Maybe he decided I'm not worth the trouble, or that I'm a pain in the ass.

Defeated and giving up on Phillip returning to his place in my office, I sigh heavily, trying not to take it personally even though I know it is.

He can't stand me and he isn't coming back.

My eyes stray to the lint brush I brought in for him, and my mouth turns down, imagining what his reaction would have been had he shown up today. Amused, entertained.

Charmed?

Who wouldn't fall a little bit in love with the girl who brought you cream cheese, followed by a sticky lint brush—a girl you discover is a veritable treasure trove of unexpected offerings! Kind of like a cat bringing its owner a dead mouse.

My shoulders hunch as I pretend to work, my attempts at productivity shot. Keeping my eyes on the work I'm fake-doing, it's late morning when Phillip surprises me. Strolls in, the baby blue button-down dress shirt a good indication that he must have had a meeting.

He came back! He doesn't hate me!

My heart races as he stops in his tracks, brown leather shoes skidding to a halt on the dark industrial carpet when he spies the lint brush offering at the same time my eyes do a sweep of his dark slacks.

Pressed pants and not jeans? What kind of meeting could it have been?

Phillip removes the lint brush before sitting, expression neutral as he finally flops down in his chair. Adjusts the chair's height—as he did yesterday—before settling in.

He nods toward the white and green sticky brush. "I don't know if I should thank you or be insulted," he states, tugging a file out of his laptop bag.

I consider this. "Probably a bit of both, actually." There's a giant long John donut on my desk and I offer him half. "Want some?"

"No thanks, I had a late breakfast."

Hmm.

"Business breakfast?"

"Yes."

Hmm.

"Where?"

He looks over at me from across the mega-desk, straight-lipped and serious. "Spencer, remember that rule about keeping the noise level down?"

"No." I chomp down on one end of the donut, chewing thoughtfully, a pencil dangled between the fingers of my other hand. I twirl it like a tiny baton, a skill I mastered in grade school when I mastered *actual* baton twirling, after begging my mother to enroll me in classes.

Baton twirling: a lost art.

Also: completely useless, unless you happen to be dating a guy with a circus fetish, which I did back in college. I would squeeze into my old leotard and perform for him, which always led to sex.

'Cause—hello—I'm so good at it.

Sex and twirling, that is.

Phillip watches the pencil go round and round my index finger, propelled by my thumb, seemingly transfixed by the motion.

"How could you have forgotten? We made the rules yesterday."

I chew and ponder, ponder and chew. "There is no rule about keeping the noise level down, and I'm not making any noise. I'm eating."

"You're being nosey, and we have an agreement about making small talk. It's distracting." He's quiet a few moments before adding, "And it's unproductive."

I glance down at his desk, where nothing is open. Nothing is on, nothing has been started. "You're not working on anything —all you've done is take that red folder out of your purse."

I use the word *purse* purposefully, knowing it's going to piss him off. Insult his masculinity and all that macho bull crap.

Phillip's nostrils flare.

Bingo! A direct hit.

"I just walked in the door—it takes longer than two minutes to get a project started." He seems to be glaring holes into my cute, pink, cashmere sweater. It's light pink and soft as cotton candy with a small, embroidered red heart over where my own beats rapidly. A hot pink pencil skirt and matching pumps are a bit much for the office on a Wednesday, but they're fun. Flirty. Sexy. A veritable Valentine's Day covering my bod.

I rack my brain for something to say.

A reason for me to rise from my desk and walk out, giving him an opportunity to see how amazing my legs look in this skirt.

Ugh, I'm such a girl.

One with a developing crush on the office sourpuss.

Fishing for a boyfriend in the workplace pond is by far the worst idea I've ever had. Is it stopping me from flirting my perky tits off?

Not one bit.

I can't help but notice his eyes quickly darting to my amazing rack, and I'm not even mad about it.

I puff out my chest and clear my throat, because despite him trying to silence me, I'd like to hear what he has to say. What stupid shit he is going to word-vomit back at me about rules and restrictions. As if the thought of tolerating me for three more days is sheer torture, so much so that he's erecting walls and creating boundaries.

Or...

Maybe, just maybe, he finds me so irresistible he can't help himself, and he knows it's unprofessional to lust after me in the office.

Yeah right.

I actually laugh out loud, knowing that's not the case.

Phillip does indeed think I'm annoying, thinks I'm too talkative, a distraction—and not the good kind.

I frown.

I'm adorable. Everyone loves me!

"Hey, nothing against you personally," Phillip begins, reading my mind. "I'm just not used to working in the same space as someone, let alone someone so..."

Pretty? Cute? Sexy? "Creative?"

His dark brows go up. "Chatty."

Chatty? How dare he! I'm just being polite!

I make a *hmph* sound and cross my arms. "You're spoiled and not used to sharing. Your dumb rules don't have anything to do with me being chatty." I spin my desk chair to face the window. He can talk to my back, *thank you very much.*

One second later, I spin back so I can look at his dumb face. "Furthermore, I'm making small talk to be *polite.*"

He holds up the lint brush as if to say, *Exhibit A: this goes beyond polite. You brought me a present, which is essentially bribery.*

So I like greasing palms—big deal.

"That is not a gift. You shed. I don't need you getting hair on everything—the chairs are black and I'm allergic," I grumble childishly.

"You're allergic to dogs?"

"I'm allergic to fashion emergencies and wardrobe malfunctions."

Then he does the one thing I'm least expecting him to do: tips his head back and laughs, a loud, raucous sound that does strange things to my insides and makes the warmth between my legs a few degrees warmer.

"It's not funny," I grumble some more as he laughs a little harder. His deep, sexy chuckle rumbles through my office.

"You're ridiculous."

"Pfft. You think I've never been called that before? Get in line, buddy." I swivel in my chair again, determined to ignore him this time. For good.

Suck it Phillip. Suck my di—

"Don't pout," he says, laughter still lacing his speech. "Baby."

"Excuse me?" It's impossible not to spin around and face my nemesis for the second time. He wants to call me names? Fine. "Do you think I was looking forward to having someone in my office, with all their shit? No. I wasn't. But I'm a team player, and I was hoping you'd at least be tolerable." I inhale. "Turns out, you're just a jerk." I pause. "It's killing my buzz."

He seems to consider this, lips curled into a tight smile. "You have a buzz?" Phillip pulls a few sheets of paper out of his red folder then continues, his question apparently having been rhetorical. "But I'm not here to make friends, or gossip, or spend my day yammering. I'm here to work. I don't know how they do it on the south side of this building, but on the north side, we don't fuck around half the day."

My mouth falls open at that last pronouncement, at the word *fuck* rolling off his tongue.

Testosterone overload much? It probably smells like Old Spice and beef jerky over there on the construction side. Dick swinging and pissing contests, men acting like assholes, trying to be more alpha than the next idiot.

Nonetheless, my cheeks flush with embarrassment. "Fine. I'll leave you alone."

"Stop talking then."

How rude!

I huff, spinning away from him for the third time so he can work on whatever groundbreaking, *super*-important stuff he has in that busted-up red folder. Out comes a pencil, out comes a power cord. Earbuds. Black-framed glasses.

I sneak a quick peek over my shoulder as he pulls out a yellow steno pad, biting back a groan.

A steno pad? My grandfather uses those.

I face the window as Phillip begins taking notes.

Know how I know he's taking notes without having to see it? Because I can *hear* the sound of lead being pressed into the paper with an unnecessarily heavy hand. He's pressing the pencil so hard the lead actually *squeaks*.

"Oh my God," I push out tersely, mostly under my breath, when I simply cannot stand the sound any longer.

The sound stops. "*What?*"

If I were wearing glasses, this is where I would whip them off as I turn to face him, like a defense attorney. "Must you press so hard on your damn pencil? Could it be any louder?"

"Now you're telling me how to write?" He's disgusted.

"No. I'm telling you it's obnoxious and asking can you please stop pushing the pencil into the paper so hard? You've probably etched through to the desk."

"You're insane." He shakes his head.

I'm insane? Umm...

"Your pencil is driving me nuts!"

"Oh, my pencil is driving you nuts." It's a statement, not a question, Phillip's tone flat and bored.

"Yes! It's offensive."

"My pencil is *offen*sive?"

"Stop repeating everything I say."

"Get over yourself." Phillip snorts, going back to note-taking, lead squeaking with every stroke. He holds the pencil up and stares at it, as if seeing it for the first time, pleased with it, and himself. "Huh. It really *is* loud."

After that, he's louder than before, a sadistic smile on his face that I want to smack right off.

He's enjoying this, that bastard.

I thrum my fingers on the desk, thinking. What would drive him nuts? Music? Chewing?

I click-click to close the windows on my desktop, rise from my desk, grab my wallet, push my chair in, and hold my head high as I saunter past him. Head straight for the breakroom, not caring any longer if he's watching me in my sexy pencil skirt.

* * *

PHILLIP

IF SHE DOESN'T STOP THAT, I'M GOING TO LOSE MY freaking mind.

Crunch.

Crunch.

Crunch.

Spencer bites into what can only be described as the crunchiest chip on the planet, created solely to make me go insane bit by bit. She slowly licks the cheese off her fingers after every chip like she did with her orange yesterday.

Doesn't even have the courtesy to use a napkin.

"Are you doing that on purpose?"

Spencer licks her lips rather than her fingers, presumably to get the salt off. Leaves them moist and glistening.

My eyes go to that bottom lip, pinker than it was earlier, and I'm not sure if it's lipstick or the salty snack that's produced that rosy shade.

"Doing what on purpose?" Her eyes are a bit too wide to be innocent.

"Eating chips." Loudly.

I have no idea where she procured a bag that size in this building, but it's huge, and when she holds it up, I notice the words FAMILY SIZE on the side. Spencer glances into its depths.

"These chips?"

"Yes." I grind my teeth, the concrete budget laid out in front of me long forgotten.

"Is there a law against me eating food in my *own office?*" The last two words come out haltingly—as if she's daring me to say so.

"No, but it's rude."

Her chin tilts. "Your *pencil* is rude."

My pencil is rude? I snort. "Of all the asinine things to say."

"Asinine," she repeats. "Jesus, who are you, your grandfather?"

Lighten up, Phillip. You really are starting to sound like a boring, old man.

Perturbed by my own irritation—and her crunching—I take a single sheet of yellow, lined paper and set it on my desk. Slowly drag my pencil across, the unhurried friction emitting a dull screech.

Spencer takes a handful of chips and shoves them in her pie hole, chomping with her mouth open, orange pieces of various sizes falling from her mouth and onto the carpet. Her desk. Her pink sweater.

Her tits.

The tight garment makes them look supple and soft and squishy and *why am I looking? Do I want her to file a complaint for harassment, for fuck's sake?*

I drop my eyes from her chest as my lead drags.

Her chips chomp and crunch.

Drag.

Chomp.

Drag. Chomp.

"Hi! Hello." A woman appears in the threshold of Spencer's office, scowling, a stack of plans in her arms. "Hi. Can the two of you cool it in here? Good God, I can hear the racket from my office."

"Sorry Karen," Spencer mumbles through a mouthful of cheesy corn chips, debris still casually falling from her pouty lips. "It's his fault."

She has no shame.

Karen stands gawking, glancing from me to Spencer. Me.

Spencer. When her scrutiny lands on me once more, it lands there long and hard, evaluating. Her hawk-like gaze narrows. "Are you from the south side?" she asks, as if she's inquiring about my gang affiliation. As if I'm from the wrong side of the tracks.

"Yes."

"That figures." Karen lets out a *hmph* before ambling away, head shaking in disgust, mumbling about manners and respect and millennials.

Spencer swallows, reaching for a bottle of water, chugs down a few mouthfuls, wipes her mouth. "Ah." She replaces the bottle top. "What a snack. Mmm mmm delicious."

I stare after the woman who just chastised us. "Who was *that*?"

"That was Karen."

"Why is she so judgy?"

"Hello, I just told you—she's a *Karen*."

I feel my face scrunch up. "Am I supposed to know what that means?"

Spencer rolls her eyes. "Guess not." She sets about ignoring me, the way I wanted her to ignore me earlier. The way I willed her to before I walked into the office this morning after my meeting. *Just let me work*, I silently prayed while riding the elevator up to the thirtieth floor. *Don't be cute, just let me work.*

Newsflash: Spencer Standish is just as sexy as she was yesterday—and she isn't letting me concentrate on work today. In fact, she isn't letting me sleep, or eat.

I lay in bed last night, staring up at the ceiling wide-eyed, listening to Humphrey saw logs. Every time I closed my eyes, I could only see my new officemate's sarcastic smile and hear her sassy laugh.

The last thing I need to be thinking about is what her body looks like without those soft, touchable clothes. A body I'll probably imagine later, covered in chip crumbles and donuts.

I'd eat stale chips off her boobs any day of the week.

I shake my head to clear the fog out of my brain. Blaine and Brooks would love this predicament I'm in—crushing on my deskmate. Tempted to flirt with her. Forcing her out of my thoughts, feigning annoyance when I actually think she's fucking adorable and irresistible.

And smart.

Sexy and so damn clever.

Yup, the guys would love this. Especially Blaine, who would win our bet if I admitted the feelings I was beginning to feel. Tingles of interest.

Sorry, Spencer—I want those baseball season tickets. Like I said, it's not personal.

Okay—it is.

"You look serious." Spencer raises one brow. "I feel a rule coming on."

"Are you suggesting one?"

She does that chin tilt I'm becoming a fan of. "I think I am."

"Okay, let's hear it."

"Rule whatever number rule we're on: no purposely being annoying to distract the other person. It's unpro*fess*ional."

"I agree." A jerky nod. "You were purposely being annoying."

Her mouth opens and closes like a mackerel. Or a bass.

"So were you." She insists on arguing, this one. Argumentative and stubborn.

"Not at first," I argue back, because I'm argumentative and stubborn. Go figure.

Spencer's hands flatten beside her keyboard and she levels me with a stare, rising up in her chair a few inches. "Are you telling me you had *no* idea your pencil was that insufferable?"

I cock my head. "I don't think an inanimate object can be insufferable."

"Agree. To. Disagree."

6

SPENCER

"Repeat after me: that guy is not worth the head space."
"That guy is not worth the head space." I do as my best friend Miranda tells me to. She works a few blocks away and meets me for lunch most days, including today. "Although, can I just say—he is *super* cute."

"Puppies are super cute. Kitties are super cute. Grown men are handsome. Or hot."

"Fine. He's handsome and hot—are you satisfied?"

"But is he a nice guy?" Miranda pushes and pushes and pushes. "I won't tolerate it if he's not a nice guy."

"Um. He might be." I wouldn't know, because all we've done is test each other's patience by arguing. "I see glimpses of nice." Not many, but a few? Like the time he… And that time…

Er.

Yeah.

Miranda takes a sip of her cappuccino. "Where does he work?"

"On the south side."

Miranda levels me with a blank stare. "I don't know what that means. I thought you just said he works for your company."

"He does. On the south side."

My friend narrows her eyes. "Speak English."

"He works on the other side of the building. If you're using a compass, it's on the south sid—"

"Okay, okay, I get it, you nerd—he's on the opposite end of the floor. Why didn't you say so in the first place?"

I thought that was what I was doing.

"It's not my fault you're directionally challenged."

It's true. Miranda will almost always get us lost if she has to drive us somewhere, not one to utilize any type of navigational system. She says they're untrustworthy and speak to her in a "tone" that doesn't sit well with her.

"Anyway," she says in an attempt to get us back on track. "What's his name?"

"Phillip."

"Phillip what?"

I shrug, dipping my adult grilled cheese sandwich into a big bowl of tomato and basil soup, then bite the sopping end off.

Mmm, so good.

"I have no idea what his last name is."

Miranda stares. "How am I supposed to social media stalk him if I don't know his last name?"

"Company directory?" I suggest, continuing to eat. The afternoon weather took a turn, and this soup combo is hitting the spot, warming me to my center. It's one of my favorite comfort foods, and I'm halfway done with the sandwich before Miranda finds Phillip on the company website.

"Phillip McGuire," she reads out loud. "Senior Buyer." My bestie glances over at me. "What does that mean?"

"Eh, I think it means he awards contracts to subcontractors and suppliers for each of the projects we're working on. Does that sound right?"

"How the hell would I know?" Miranda rolls her eyes. "I'm a jewelry designer—I work with pearls and gold, not concrete and...and..."

"Rebar? Stone? Plumbing?"

"Sure. What you said, nerd," she says. "There isn't much here, just his name and where he went to college, and how long he's been in construction."

"Let me see."

She turns her phone so I can look at Phillip McGuire in color, a blip on her small screen. Using two fingers, I enlarge the professional headshot.

Plaid shirt. Thick black hair combed to one side in a dorky cute way. Pleasant but aloof grin—as if he knew he was required to smile but wasn't feeling it at the time. I tilt my head a smidge to study it.

Actually, he looks constipated—like he had to take a shit but couldn't find a toilet.

I snicker, studying it some more.

He had the beginning of a beard in the photograph, dark and bristly. Coupled with the blue and green plaid flannel, it sends warm shivers fluttering down inside my stomach, creeping their way farther into my lady parts.

I'm a sucker for plaid and beards and agitated smiles, evidently.

Ugh.

"What's that look?" Miranda asks, sounding an awful lot like my officemate.

"I don't have a look," I object, pushing her phone away to eat more lunch.

"Yes you do. Your face is bright red."

"So? This soup is hot."

"Spencer Standish, your face is red because you're staring at his picture. You have a crush on someone at work—why won't you just admit it?"

"Because, if I say it out loud, it becomes true." Everyone knows that—it's like telling everyone your birthday wish. Or revealing what you wish for when the clock strikes 11:11. "And personally, I think dating someone from work is a horrible idea, with a capital W-H-O-R-E-I-B-L-E. Horrible."

"Need I remind you who dated Nate from the IT department at her company for two years?"

"Yeah—and who had to quit when the company found out?"

"Nate?"

"Exactly."

"Okay, but we had a no-fraternization policy. You don't."

"We don't?" I crane my neck to glance at the microscopic words on her phone.

"No, I just checked and couldn't find anything in the online manual for potential new employees. You can have your cake and eat it too."

I push the soup around with my spoon and consider the question. "That's only because the CEO of my company has been dating his secretary since his wife found out he was banging his secretary."

"*Hello*, this all works out in your favor."

"First of all, Phillip McGuire does not want to date me."

Miranda sips her own soup, wipes her mouth, then rolls her eyes. "And second of all?"

"Second of all, he might not even be single. He could be married."

"You seriously think he's married? How old is this guy?"

"My age?" There's a good chance he's in a relationship. "Possibly."

"Has he *said* anything about a wife? Or a girlfriend?"

I give her a look. "Miranda, he isn't going to tell me he has a girlfriend. We just met—you ease into information like that." Besides, he isn't one for idle chitchat, made a rule about small talk, and the whole corn chip/pencil debacle put him over the edge. When I left for lunch today, Phillip blatantly ignored me, and if my eyes weren't deceiving me, his body visibly relaxed when I passed him on my way out the door.

If he's attracted to me, he's doing a terrible job of showing it.

Tall, brawny, masculine Phillip—the quintessential man's

man, and not so much of a metrosexual. Unexpected in a city like Chicago, where most guys try too hard to fit in, to be too modern, or are just as fake as women can be when they're single and trying to mingle.

Single.

Kind of wish I knew if he was or not so I could tone down or ramp up the flirting accordingly. It wouldn't do to embarrass myself over someone who isn't available.

Not that it's stopped me before.

7

PHILLIP

I pause in the doorway of Spencer's office, rendered immobile by the sight of a grilled cheese sandwich on my desk.

I love grilled cheese.

I'm trying not to love Spencer.

Slowly, I shuffle my way inside, back from the restroom and a quick lap around the breakroom on a hunt for lunch that turned up empty.

Nothing appetizing.

It's half past one in the afternoon, so the starvation game is strong—and wouldn't you know it? Grilled cheese happens to be one of my all-time favorite things in the whole wide world. It's in a Styrofoam container, with a white, covered cardboard bowl next to it, and I'm hoping and praying it's soup for dipping.

"Where did this come from?" I ask, a bit suspiciously, removing my laptop from the desk and resting it on the floor to create more room. I grab one half of the sandwich, palming it; the thick bread is packed with cheese, sliced diagonally.

I bite down.

It's still warm.

Ooey, gooey delicious cheese (which will probably give me gas later, but right now, my stomach does not care).

"It came from me." Spencer's voice is small as she briefly glances up with a hesitant smile, finally clicking away at her own keyboard.

"Did you make this?" I ask dumbly, for lack of anything better to say.

"No, silly. I went to lunch and brought one back."

"How did you know I love grilled cheese?" I moan through a mouthful of bread and melted dairy.

"I didn't. That's what *I* had for lunch, and I just ordered another one for you before I left."

I glance at the sandwich while I chew. "Why?"

Spencer sighs as if the answer is obvious. "Because you came in late, and you didn't leave for lunch when I left for lunch. I had a feeling you wouldn't, and I noticed you only eat food that's provided in the breakroom, thought you might enjoy a sandwich."

Whoa.

Okay.

"That was…" I pause, unsure. "Nice."

"Is that so hard for you to say?" Spencer laughs as she moves the mouse for her computer around its pad. "Don't sound so put out about it or I won't bring you food. Not if you don't want me to."

My stomach is affronted by the mere suggestion, and I'm hasty to reply, "No—I appreciate it. It was nice."

She flips her long, dark hair. "I know."

Dammit!

"It was nine bucks," she informs me as she begins clicking open files on her desktop. "So, *yeah*."

"I'll pay you back."

"All I'm saying is, don't puke it up in the garbage." Spencer spins in her chair in an attempt to get the last word in before presenting me with her back. "It wasn't cheap."

Great. Now I have to choke it down with that on my mind

while she watches me devour the damn thing, waiting for me to vomit the whole meal into the trash.

My stomach growls again, warning me against idle chitchat. *Less talking, more eating*, it grumbles.

"Did you do something to this?" I eyeball the sandwich skeptically, though it tastes fine and not at all like it's been poisoned. "It's safe to eat, right? No arsenic?"

Spencer swivels in her chair to glare at me. "Why would I do something like that? My goal is to stay out of prison."

"So you can watch me puke into the garbage?"

She laughs, tipping her head back. "That does sound like something I would do."

"See?" Still, none of this stops me from devouring the offering. I remove the lid from the white container—surprise, surprise, she did bring me soup!—and proceed to dip my grilled cheese.

It's raining outside, and the temperature has dropped below fifty, so the combo platter is the perfect lunch. I savor it, especially since I also didn't have to pay for it myself, a novel concept. No one ever buys me lunch! I am always the one paying, especially when I'm with my cheap-ass friends. Everyone gets alligator arms when the check comes to the table, and I'm typically the one stuck paying.

Speaking of my friends, I have a bro date with them tonight, a quick drop-in for drinks to catch up since we've rarely seen one another lately, ever since Brooks went and got himself relationshipped.

Unlucky bastard.

He swears he's happy, but how can he be having lost the bet and his sweet, sweet season tickets? He loved those tickets more than life itself, but apparently not more than he loves his girlfriend Abbott. Losing had to have hurt—I know I'd be sulking if those tickets had been mine. Brooks, on the other hand? He's taking it pretty well. Says the love of a great woman is worth it and he would give them up all over again if it meant finding Abbott.

I'll be the first to admit, Abbott is a badass chick, and I probably don't judge him too harshly for falling in love. She's gorgeous, adorable in her own way, and loveable. Not at all annoying like my deskmate for the week.

I glance up.

Spencer is straight-up studying me as I attack this sandwich like a fucking caveman, dark brows in the hairline above her smooth skin. Her long lashes flutter occasionally, just enough to let me know she's still breathing.

Why is it so hard to tell if she's amused or disgusted?

Does it matter?

Nope.

I can't date her.

I tear off a hunk of the second half of the sandwich, grateful it was made on huge slices of thick sourdough bread, and I chomp, cheese dripping down my chin.

Dip it in the soup, sopping up the tomato base, then go at it again.

Dip. Chomp. Dip. Chomp.

"You really are a caveman," Spencer says, reading my mind.

A caveman who didn't have to go scavenging for food. All I have to do is smile at her and she's bringing me shit. Not a bad day on the job.

I immediately feel guilty.

"I said thank you," I remind her, although I didn't actually say thank you. "Thanks."

We settle into a companionable silence after that, her clicking away with her mouse as she moves it around the pad, me scarfing down lunch and checking emails on my phone.

A snack appears on my desk when I return from taking a piss around four o'clock, and I feel like sharing this office won't be the worst thing that's happened to me all year. It's a giant chocolate chip cookie and plain granola, and I doubt it's from the breakroom.

Satisfied from lunch, the treats, and the contracts we've been awarded for the project I've been bidding, I text Humphrey's dog walker to see if she can pop in and play with him and take him potty. Since I didn't make it to the office until later, looks like I'm going to stay a bit later, at least until I meet the Bastards for a drink. No sense in racing home, letting the dog out, then racing back to this part of town if it can be avoided.

The dog walker is available. She usually is since that's her main gig and she's always up for the extra cash, and let me tell you—it isn't cheap having someone else come take Humphrey for a walk.

But he likes her, and it eases my burden so I can push through at work and get shit done.

Anyway.

Back to the snacks on my desk.

The plastic baggie of granola is big and hearty, so I suspect it isn't store-bought. But I could be wrong. "Did you make this?" I hold up an almond and inspect it with one eye squinted shut. It looks baked and smells delicious.

I pop it in my mouth and chew.

"Yeah, I made a batch this past weekend." Spencer is still working, one earbud in, the other dangling down her chest so she can hear me.

"You made this?"

Now she turns to face me. "You sound surprised."

"I am." I scoop a handful into my gullet and savor the cinnamon and sugar she has sprinkled on it, the raisins. "It's so good." Better than the sandwich she fed me for lunch. "If you keep feeding me, you're gonna have to drag me out of here kicking and screaming," I warn with a grin.

From here, it looks like Spencer is blushing—but I could be wrong. The sun is beaming in from behind her and the glare is blinding. "Aw, I'm sure your girlfriend would hate it if she heard you refusing to leave."

Whoa.

Hold up.

Is she fishing for information? Is that her not-so-subtle way of asking if I have a girlfriend? Better bring the hammer down so she lowers her expectations.

"I don't have a girlfriend, and I'm not looking for one."

There. Too harsh, but also the truth.

"I wasn't asking," she lies prettily, avoiding my gaze to stare at her computer monitor. "I assumed you had one, so... Whatever."

More food goes into my mouth. "Why would you assume I'm in a relationship?"

Spencer stops what she's doing long enough to shrug, give me a glance, and bite down on her lower lip. "You look like the type."

I look like the type?

Literally not a single person has ever said that about me—at least not to my face—and I doubt anyone ever will. Spencer Standish is full of shit and we both know it. I do not, in fact, look like the relationship type, and she was indeed fishing for information about me.

She knows I'm the consummate bachelor.

I know it.

I'm such a confirmed bachelor I have a blue velvet smoking jacket, for fuck's sake. How douchey is that? A jacket I'm seriously considering having my initials embroidered on just to drive home my single status on the nights my friends and I wear them in public.

My fingers flex, itching to feel that fabric.

The jacket is with me at work.

Yeah. I brought it. Stuffed it into my laptop bag, folded into a neat little square, probably getting horribly wrinkled.

Shit. I should probably take it out of my bag so it's not a

mess by the time I need to wear it later tonight. It won't do to be the only asshole at the meeting with a wrinkly jacket.

It would only make me look like an even bigger douche than I'll already be.

Swallowing the granola in my mouth, I lean over and unzip my laptop bag, fingering the smooth, velvety square tucked inside. Grasp it and pull, giving it a little shake when it's loose from the bag. Twist my body to hang it on the back of my desk chair, out of Spencer's sight.

"What's that?"

Too fucking late. "Don't you have work to do?"

Why is she constantly watching me? Nosey little shit.

"I am working, but your desk is so close you're constantly up my asshole. Forgive me for noticing when you take something out of your purse."

Up her asshole? My *purse*?

What the...

Who talks like that? Spencer, apparently—that's who.

Jeez, this girl is certifiable.

Not in an insane way, just—a pain-in-my-ass kind of way. Her saucy mouth is weirdly turning me on, and I hate it.

Fuck.

"How about you mind your own business for once?"

"Um, hello—need I remind you that this is my office?"

"Um, hello," I repeat. "You're incessantly reminding me that this is your office. And trust me, as soon as I get the green light, I'm so out of here." I root around in the bag for more granola, stuff it in my mouth.

"You literally just got done saying they'd have to drag you out of here kicking and screaming!"

"I lied," I lie.

"It's not stopping you from enjoying the perks, though, is it? Freeloader."

"Excuse me?" I ask through a full mouth of warm cookie.

A crumb chooses that moment to fall on my shirt, traitorous little bastard.

"If I'm so terrible, maybe you shouldn't eat the lunch I bring you. And keep your mitts off my snacks." She arches a brow and extends her hand in my direction across her desk. "Give that back."

I shake my head, holding the baggie and the cookie to my chest. "No."

"I said, give it back!"

"It's mine. You gave it to me."

"I gave it to you as a gesture of *goodwill*, and you don't even appreciate it!"

So? I'm a guy—of course I appreciate her gesture, but I'm not going to get all gushy over it. I'm not a chick. I'll only gush over amazing sex, and maybe a trip I don't have to organize myself. Those are the only things that warrant a good slobbery gush-fest, and both almost never happen.

I shove more into my face, the granola falling down the front of my shirt the way Spencer's chips did yesterday. "If you want this back, you're going to have to come over here and physically remove it from my dead, lifeless hands."

"That can be arranged." Her pretty eyes narrow into dangerous slits—dangerous, sexy slits, I might add. Spencer Standish is hot when she's being cunning.

I ignore her.

I ignore her when she prattles on, and I ignore her when she goes stealthily quiet.

A move that costs me when she rises from her seat—I'm shoving granola into my esophagus and barely paying her any attention at this point—and her hand yanks at the jacket hanging on the back of my chair.

"Fuck!" I spit out everything I was gnawing on. "Give that back!"

"Come and get it," she taunts, but not before eyeing up the

garment. Runs her fingers along the expensive stitching, the delicate trim, the silk lining inside. "What the hell is this?"

"None of your business," I tell her for the second time today. "Nonyo. Biznass."

"But now I'm invested." She holds it up and out of my reach as I lurch forward, attempting to snatch it back.

"You can have the granola." I take the bag and toss it onto her desk.

"Mm, don't want it anymore." She's plainly curious about the jacket. Even sniffs it. "Do you wear this? Like, this fits you?" Her eyes scan me up and down. "It doesn't match your outfit."

Excuse me? "Yes it does." Not that it matters, but the jacket matching my outfit hardly matters. It's the jacket itself that matters if I want to attend a meeting of the Bastard Bachelor Society. Kind of a thing we're all sticklers about.

No jacket, no drink.

And most of the reason we meet is to bitch and complain about our day.

The jacket is a symbol of our brotherhood, our friendship. Sometimes we smoke cigars, sometimes we just talk, always at The Basement.

"Who wears velvet anymore?"

"Lots of people."

The famous tilt of her chin. "Name some."

I can't name a single one, unless you count my mom during the holidays. Vicky McGuire loves her some black velvet skirts during Christmas. And Prince. He definitely liked velvet.

I do not mention my mother; Spencer would make fun of me. Nor do I mention Prince, because it would be ludicrous to compare myself to a pop star.

Instead, I cross my arms and roll my eyes. "Give me the jacket."

"Can I try it on?"

"No!" I shout, a little too loudly. She should know better

than to even ask; I'm trying to get the damn thing out of her grasp—why would I allow her to try it on?

"Rawr, someone is getting testy over a dumb jacket."

"It's not a dumb jacket," I grumble, a sound I've made at least half a dozen times since moving my shit into Spencer's office. Funny how I'm never this bitchy on the south side. Maybe it's the lack of testosterone in here.

Maybe I need to pack up my shit and go.

I look up into Spencer's puppy dog eyes and pouty bottom lip.

Sigh.

I mean—what's the worst thing that could happen if I let her try on the jacket? It's not like anyone would find out about it...

"Fine."

"Fine? Fine as in yes I can try it on?"

I sigh again. Louder this time, for dramatic effect. "Yes—but do it fast, and don't linger, and take it off immediately."

I'm already regretting this. Such a bad idea.

"You are so weird, Phillip McGuire."

Lately, yeah.

I watch as Spencer shrugs her narrow shoulders into my navy jacket. It's large on her, but the color is flattering and—what the hell am I talking about? *Flattering?* Jesus.

She pulls the lapels closed and purses her lips, posing. Fluffs her hair and makes a show of twirling in circles. "I could wear this as a dress, belted off with cute heels," she tells me. The last thing I want to picture is her prancing around in nothing but my jacket with bare legs and stilettos.

"Time to take it off," I chastise like a fuddy-duddy, giving her the 'gimme' motion with my hand. "Give it up, Standish."

"Aww," she croons, shrugging it off as easily as she pulled it on. "You know my last name."

I shake my head. "Don't flatter yourself—it's on your desk." And it is, on a nameplate she has sitting front and center, brown wood grain with gold etched letters. The kind of sign you have made yourself when you've been promoted and have your very own office, when you want to feel important.

I should know—I have one just like it on my desk. I had it made at the mall, at a kiosk, when I was promoted and got moved from a cubicle to my very own office.

Spencer Standish.

Has a nice ring to it.

She hands my jacket back, leaning across our monolith of a desk, our hands brushing when I grasp the velvet. I don't intend to, but I tingle.

Fuck if I don't...

8

SPENCER

"What's he doing with a blue velvet smoking jacket?" Miranda wants to know, staring at me through the lens on her phone, one hand gripping a train rail, the loud sounds of the engine and people surrounding her almost drowning her out.

Her phone rocks and shakes as she stands in the L train at the end of the day, our afternoon ritual of FaceTiming uninterrupted despite her being on the go.

"I have no idea." I'm already home, and I prop my feet up on the coffee table, already in slippers, already in pajamas, already forking a giant bowl full of buttered rice.

I'm too lazy to cook anything healthy, too cheap to order takeout or delivery.

"How are you going to find out?" Miranda is yelling, and I cannot imagine what the other passengers are thinking. Probably want to kill her, or muzzle her. Or both. Nothing is more annoying than someone on their phone in public, worse when they're video-chatting with someone.

Ugh.

So glad I don't have to put up with it. I would want to smack her.

"You could just ask," my best friend suggests.

"As if he'd tell me what it's for? Please. You should have seen him when I asked if I could put it on." I laugh. "Better yet, you should have seen the fool's face when I snatched it from him."

Gotta be quick, gotta be quick if you're going to get it back from me...

"Men," Miranda says, and I imagine she's chuckling, because that's what Miranda does: finds humor in everything.

"He should have known I was going to try to steal it. What an amateur." I laugh again. "It did smell good, though."

"Which means he probably hasn't washed it from the last time he wore it."

I hadn't thought of that. "I mean—it seems like it's for special occasions? Velvet? I doubt he ran a marathon in it, 'cause it didn't stink—it's not like his gym clothes, stop judging."

It smelled like aftershave and man and handsomeness. Mmm mmm *mmm.*

"What are you eating?" my friend wants to know, nosey as ever, even on a train.

I hold up my bowl so she can inspect it.

"Rice? That's it?"

"I'm lazy," I tell her, as if it weren't obvious.

"You should meet me out for dinner."

"I'm already in my pajamas," I remind her, turning the camera so she can see my fuzzy pink pants and gray fuzzy slippers that look like mice, complete with cute little ears, pink noses, and whiskers.

"You have makeup on, and you can eat the bar olives from my martini," she allows. "You love doing that."

It's true; I do love eating the olives when Miranda gets drinks. For some reason, they taste better when they're not from your cocktail.

"I could I guess. Throw on jeans and a sweater..."

"That's the spirit," my best friend whoops, and over her

shoulder, I see a few people roll their eyes. "Where should we go? Let's find a new spot—I'm tired of the downtown scene."

Fine with me. I'm in no mood for doing the after-work, happy hour grind with the other pathetic singles in the metro area. I'm over it. "Where can we go where it's kind of quiet but we can get a decent sandwich and a good cocktail?"

We think on it.

I watch as Miranda leans over to strike up a conversation with some hot guy reading a novel, but I can't hear what she asks him or what he's saying in response.

"This guy said there's a place called The Basement that's low-key but real nice. It's on my end of town."

"Yeah, that's fine—I'll just hop in a cab."

"I'm almost to my stop—don't really want to go home and change," she tells me, hoisting her shoulder bag to redistribute the weight. "Forty-five minutes?"

"At The Basement?"

"Yup."

"Cool, cool. See you then."

9

PHILLIP

"How's married life?" Our friend Blaine is the first person to speak when we're all sitting down, at the spot in The Basement we've established as our own. During the week, it's a crapshoot whether our special seats will be available, and tonight, we're in luck, because all three of them are.

Plus, the bartender who occasionally gives us free appetizers is here.

Score.

"Yeah, tell us how Abbott is," I add before Brooks can get defensive about his relationship status. He and his girlfriend are shacking up together, so it's pretty serious, although he likes to occasionally pretend otherwise.

Tonight is no such occasion. "Fucking great," he says with a wink and a nod, his toothy grin saying what his mouth isn't. He's happy and content, in it for the long haul.

I mean, think about it—the guy gave up a lot to be with his girlfriend. Oh, he fought it pretty damn hard, lying to us about all the time they were spending together and the fact that they'd fallen in love, but eventually, he couldn't stand the secrets and the truth came spilling out.

"Don't get me wrong, sometimes it's a huge pain in the ass

living with her, but that's only because I've never done it before, and I still don't trust the cat."

His girlfriend has an evil cat named Desdemona that used to hiss and take swipes at him.

The Pussy of Terror, he called it.

Brooks adjusts the cuffs on his blue smoking jacket—a jacket he had to give back to us when he broke the club rules, fell in love, let his neighbor-girl-turned-girlfriend wear his club coat, and told her about the Bastard Bachelor Society.

Blaine and I decided to let him wear it. Because we're cool like that. Plus, he whined about it like a baby.

I sit idly, not mentioning the fact I let Spencer in my office try mine on today. The thought makes me feel ill. And guilty.

I take a swig of my drink and avert my eyes.

Clear my throat. "How's work?"

Our friend is an architect totally killing it at his new job with a promotion and new office.

"Can't complain. Long hours, lots of stress." He takes a drink from his glass, too, then chases it with a handful of almonds. "It's nice having someone to come home to, and I'm not talking about Desi."

Yeah, I know what he means. It's nice coming home to Humphrey, even if he is just a dog.

Just a dog? Also my best buddy.

Fucking Humphrey.

The dog walker sent me a few Snaps of their walk to the park, and for once in his damn life, the hound managed to behave his damn self. Why does he make it easy for her but hell for me?

Damn dog. He knows *exactly* what he's doing.

"How are you boys doing?" He gives me a pointed look. "Didn't you say they were tearing up the floor at your office?"

"Carpet. And yeah, it's in shambles right now. Should be done on Friday though, then they start on the north side."

It hasn't occurred to me until just now that there's a good

possibility Spencer will be in my office when they start remodeling hers.

"What a pain in the ass." He rubs the stubble on his chin. "You had to move your shit into someone else's office, right? How's that going?"

"Fine." I shift in my seat, uncomfortable. If I tell them I'm officing with a female, they'll get all weird and start asking inappropriate questions.

Like *Is she hot?* And *Is she single?* And *Does she seem interested?*

Yes, I don't know, and—*maybe.*

Not that it matters, because I cannot date anyone.

Not if I want those season tickets...

"So they just shoved another desk into each office?" Blaine wants to know.

"Pretty much."

"Why didn't they just let you work from home for the week?"

I shrug. "Couldn't say."

"That would be nice," Brooks agrees. "But you wouldn't get jack shit done."

And I wouldn't be able to stare at Spencer when she isn't looking, or have her feed me when I step out to hit the bathroom only to find a snack on my chair when I return.

I'm bound to get spoiled.

Am already.

And it's only been two full days.

"Who is your officemate? Some dork from accounting?" Blaine asks rudely, forgetting the fact that he is an accountant.

"No."

"Human resources? That would be hilarious—they can't write you up for being a douche if they're sharing an office with you." Brooks laughs.

"Very funny." I take a drink to avoid answering, almost choking when I catch sight of Spencer Standish and another female pausing in the entrance of The Basement, both of them scanning the area. Casing the joint.

The girl next to Spencer nudges her with an elbow, and they walk in farther as I shrink down in my seat to delay the inevitable: her spotting me and coming over.

Because if she sees me, she will.

That's just the kind of person Spencer is. Balls to the wall, meets things head on, doesn't avoid conflict kind of girl.

Fuck, fuck, fuck.

I choke a little, sputtering.

"What the hell is wrong with you?" Brooks asks, his entire face scrunched up, staring at me like I'm crazy.

"Nothing. I just…"

We're all sitting here like assholes wearing matching jackets, and if she comes over here—what if she tells them she tried mine on today?

Fuck, fuck, fuckity fuck.

Shit balls. "Is it hot in here? Maybe we should take these off." I suggest, hoping they'll follow my lead.

"Take these off? We're in session—you have to wear the jacket." Yeah, they definitely think I'm acting nuts.

I shrink down farther, ass almost to the edge of the seat, head barely rising above the back of the chair.

"Why are you acting weird?" Blaine is more intuitive than he lets on, and he glances around the bar area. "Do you see someone you know?"

"No!" It comes out too loud and too frantic, and he knows I'm lying.

"Is ittt…" He's intent on discovering Spencer's identity, and he looks straight at her and her companion. "That girl? The blonde?"

Definitely not the blonde, but close enough. I need him not to make a scene, and I consider hauling ass to the bathroom—and staying there. I can shove some nuts in my pocket to hold me over.

"Who are we looking at?" Now Brooks is in on the action, neck craning, eyes scanning, mouth gaping.

I am so screwed.

"Would you knock it off?" I try to say it casually but have never managed to pull that off, not even as a teenager when my mother was embarrassing me. Like my friends are right now.

"She's not even looking—calm your tits." Brooks rolls his eyes. Easy for him to say; he's not the one who has to show his face at the office in the morning.

"No, but she will be." Blaine's hand shoots up and he waves it, catching the attention of Spencer's friend. They look over.

I can see the range of emotion crossing over Spencer's face, can read her body language, even from here. She is feeling the same things I am: excitement and dread, both at the same time.

"Don't," her lips are telling the other girl, holding her arm back as her friend slowly begins weaving her way over to our dysfunctional little party, smug smile on her face that matches that of my bastard buddies. She's the female version of Brooks and Blaine: cocky, arrogant, and attractive.

"Hi!" the friend is saying as they approach, Spencer lagging behind like an adolescent being humiliated by her parent, a blush on her cheeks that glows as bright as her teal blue sweater.

"Phillip and my friend here work together." She's chipper and cheery and I don't trust her one bit, especially when she gives Spencer a tiny shove forward.

"Imagine that, boys! Phillip works with this pretty young lady and didn't tell us." Brooks kicks me in the shin. "Sit up straight, son. Your manners suck."

I sit up straight, coming off like a complete fucking tool.

Do I say hi? Do I wait for her to say hi? Jesus, why is this so awkward? I work with Spencer; it's not like I'm interested in her —yet here I sit, tongue-tied.

Is it because I'm attracted to her and it's taboo? That has nothing to do with anything. That should not turn me into a bumbling moron in public. I've been attracted to way prettier girls before and done just fine.

Shit.

That came out all wrong in my brain. That's not how I meant it. My point is, I'm cooler than this, for God's sake.

"Hey." I nod at Spencer, accompanying my stellar salutation with a stilted wave.

"Hey!" Spencer is cherry red and seems to have found her personality—after being forcibly dragged over here. "Weird bumping into you here, of all places. Do you come here often?"

How the hell did she hear about this place? It's dominated by men—or maybe that's the reason she's here? Is Spencer looking for a hookup? A relationship? If she is, it would make sense to come to The Basement; not a bar in town with more male testosterone per square foot.

"It's our spot," Brooks tells her, reaching up to offer his hand for a shake. "I'm Brooks, by the way, since Dipshit there has forgotten his manners. And that's our buddy Blaine."

Spencer's blue eyes go from me to Brooks to Blaine, and then to our matching jackets.

Her brows go up, and I pray she doesn't say a word about it. *Please don't ask, please don't ask...*

"I'm Spencer, and this is Miranda." She pauses, staring at Blaine's jacket. Raises her eyes. "Phillip and I work together."

Both bastards turn toward me. "What a coincidence that you're here tonight."

Spencer shifts on her heels. "We're sharing an office this week," she adds, and I inwardly groan. "I'm not stalking you or anything—we found out about this place from a guy she knows." She thumbs toward her friend.

"Not stalking him? Bor-ing." The smirk on Brooks' face is like the cat that ate the mouse—sly and arrogant. "Though it's weird that our buddy here never mentioned you—I don't remember you telling us you were sharing an office with a girl."

"And we were specifically asking him about work today," Blaine adds helpfully, and I wish he would shut his face.

"Very specifically who his new officemate is," Brooks lies.

Spencer flushes deeper. "I mean…we just work together. It's not a big deal, not really worth mentioning. He's squatting in my office while his gets remodeled." Fidgeting while she word-vomits, Spencer plays with a long strand of hair falling over her shoulder, twisting it a few times before releasing it.

"If you were my officemate for a week, you better fucking believe I'd tell my friends about it," Brooks declares, turning to me. "Is there a reason you didn't tell your friends about it, buddy?"

I want to kill him.

I want to kill them both, seriously.

Spencer's friend—cute and flirty, wearing heels and hot pink —leisurely checks me out. Inspects me like I'm an insect, as if it's her job, scanning me from head to toe, beginning with my hair, shoulders, chest, and…everything else.

Evidently Spencer has told her friend about me.

The friend—Miranda—squints at us, though there is ample lighting in the bar. "Why are you dressed like triplets?"

"We're not," Blaine replies. "Purely coincidental."

Miranda folds her arms and leans her hip on the edge of Brooks' chair. "It's a coincidence you're all dressed like Hugh Hefner?"

Blaine nods again. "Yes, ma'am."

Clearly Miranda isn't buying it because *clearly* it's a load of crap. "Look me in the eye and tell me there isn't something else going on here. What is this, a club meeting?"

Brooks chokes on his cocktail while I begin pounding him on the back in an effort to avoid the questioning. Red-faced and panting, my best friend wipes his mouth with the sleeve of his blue velvet jacket and sits up straighter in his chair, attempting to act dignified.

"Why would you think this is a club?"

Yeah, what would make her assume that?

Both girls roll their eyes like we're idiots, but it's Spencer who finally speaks. "Because there are three of you, and you're all dressed the same? Which is super weird because you're grown-ass men—unless it's a meeting for something."

Grown-ass men.

The way she says it makes us sound immature, and only Blaine warrants that label.

Spencer tilts her head in that way I've grown familiar with, the hair on the side of her face falling away to reveal the smooth column of her neck. Long and delicate.

Ugh. Fuck.

Fuck this dumb club and this dumb bet.

It's making me look and feel like an asshole.

"Can we get you ladies a drink?" Brooks offers, and I suspect it's because he wants to change the subject, not because he's itching to have them sit with us. After all, he has a girlfriend.

"We don't want drinks, but thanks," Miranda says at the same time Spencer asks, "This isn't a fraternity thing?" Not surprising that the stubborn minx is not willing to let the subject die.

I'm going to hear about this at work, and I'm going to hear about this from the Bastards as soon as Spencer and her friend walk away. Which I wish they would, because I'm starting to sweat inside the thick fabric of this blazer.

Whose dumb idea was this club anyway? I shoot a scowl at Brooks, whose dumb idea it was—he's swirling the ice cubes in his glass and playing dumb.

"Spencer, I guess I'll see you tomorrow." There. I put an end to the conversation the only way I know how—bluntly. Rudely, even, though that's nothing out of the ordinary. With her the past few days, I've been prickly—on edge. So unlike myself I wonder if I'm going to make it through Friday.

The girls smile politely. Spencer gives a tiny wave. "It was nice meeting y'all," she tells my friends. "See you tomorrow, Phillip."

When they walk off, not one of us says a word; we don't dare. We watch as the girls head back toward the entrance of The Basement, get their jackets from coat check, and leave. I hold my breath the entire time.

Then…

"*See you tomorrow, Phillip,*" Brooks mimics in a feminine voice, sounding lovesick and sighing. "What. Was. *That* all about?"

"She did not say it like that."

"Oh no—she did. She sounded just like that." He clears his throat then goes on. "Phillip and I *work* together."

"What the fuck, dude—why didn't you tell us you were sharing an office with a chick? She's hot! How can you concentrate?"

I can't. "It's easy—she's annoying."

"Does it matter? She's gorgeous." Blaine's eyes stray toward the door and my hackles rise; I don't need him lusting after my co-worker. It feels…wrong. Especially since I'm lusting after her, too.

"She eats a lot of junk food," I fib, remembering the chip incident—though that was just to piss me off.

"Who cares?"

"Like a slob. She'll probably die at an early age from clogged arteries," I argue, building a case so he'll stop reminding me Spencer is good-looking and hot.

"She eats junk food?" Brooks isn't impressed with my excuses. "That's your big argument against her hotness?"

"And her work ethic sucks."

"How?"

"Well, she gets to the office early but doesn't actually do anything."

They both stare at me as if I've sprouted two heads.

"Her ability to be productive in the office has nothing to do with her ability to fuck," Brooks points out, raising his hand to signal the server. He orders another round with a flick of his wrist.

"She's probably messy." I can't imagine how disordered her apartment or house or whatever living quarters are, based on the fact that she leaves crumbs on the front of her sweater.

"Again—irrelevant."

Totally irrelevant. To my own ears, the arguments sound weak, but I cannot let them get the faintest whiff that I'm interested in Spencer. That I'm more and more attracted to her as the days roll by. I'd be screwed. Blaine would do whatever he could to put her in my path so I'd lose the bet.

He's no idiot, and now he smells drama...

* * *

SPENCER

Miranda: *Why does your officemate have to be so hot?*
Me: *Is he?*
Miranda: *You literally told me yesterday you thought he was good-looking and then you brought him lunch like a little puppy dog. Then you told me he makes you nervous—you were BLUSHING.*
Me: *I didn't actually think you were going to meet him in person! My bad.*
Miranda: *Well, you were wrong.*
Miranda: *By the way—he is way hotter in person than in that dorky photo on the internet.*
Me: *You didn't tell me you thought he looked dorky!*
Miranda: *I was being SUPPORTIVE. That's what friends do. Speaking of supportive, do you think his friends are single? Hook a girl up.*
Me: *Probably? They look single.*
Miranda: *The one with the brown hair didn't.*

Me: *What makes you say that?*

Miranda: *He looked like someone picks out his clothes. PLUS (and this is a big plus) he wasn't hitting on me.*

Me: *None of them were hitting on you. Or me.*

Miranda: *Don't you think that's weird??*

Me: *I guess so? Maybe? Who even knows with guys anymore. #IGiveUp*

Miranda: *Why do you suppose he didn't tell his friends about you?*

Me: *No idea. Haven't given it any thought.*

Miranda: *You're SUCH a liar! Of course you've thought about it—that's what girls do.*

Me: *He didn't tell his friends because he isn't lusting over me.*

Miranda: *False. He didn't tell his friends about you BECAUSE he is lusting after you.*

Me: *Time will tell I guess. Maybe he'll be so overcome with passion by Friday that he won't be able to stand it anymore. Fancy a hard office bang?*

Miranda: *Yes, yes, I am loving that!*

Miranda: *Also wondering—what the hell was with those matching jackets?*

Me: *I don't know, but I'm going to find out...*

10

SPENCER

I don't bring up the weird Hugh Hefner jackets he and his
friends were wearing last night. As strange as it looked, it's
something they obviously didn't want us asking about.

So I don't.

I might like to tease Phillip, but I know when to respect
boundaries. Most of the time...

Besides, I'll figure it out eventually.

We're on our third day together, both of us rushing in late
this morning. Phillip pants when he hits the threshold of the
office, laptop bag practically choking him as it hangs
haphazardly from his neck. Coat askew, all the buttons in the
wrong holes. Hair windblown.

"Trouble with Humphrey?" I glance up, having only just
arrived myself.

"He is going to be the death of me."

I giggle into the brim of my latte cup. "I feel a kinship to
this dog. You should bring him in sometime."

"No way—although I told Paul I would, but that's only
because I was kissing his ass on a day I was super fucking late."
He looks at me and cringes. "Shit. Pardon my language."

"God, don't apologize. I've heard worse. *Hello*, I work in a male-dominated industry."

When Phillip has his things organized on his side of the room, he sits, regarding me. "What's that like?"

"What's what like?"

"Working here—in a construction office?"

I consider this, having never discussed it with any of my co-workers before. I've only had this talk with my girlfriends. "At first it was an adjustment, but I'm on this side of the building, so it's mostly women." I pause before adding, "When I was first hired here, I was excited because I thought it would be exciting to work with guys, you know? I'm single and thought maybe it would be fun to meet someone here, but the reality is most of the dudes are my father's age." I give him a wink. "No offense."

Phillip rolls his eyes. "We both know I'm not anywhere near your dad's age."

"How old are you?"

"Twenty-eight. How old are you?"

"Thirty."

I watch as his eyes bug out a little at the revelation. "You're thirty? You look…" He searches for an age. "I thought you were twenty-two."

"Twenty-two! They'd never have hired me for this position fresh out of college."

He has the decency to look uncomfortable. "How the hell would I know that?"

"I guess I shouldn't be arguing with you—I should be flattered." Neatly stacking a pile of folders in my outbox, I shoot him a grin. "You really thought I was that young? Wow." My grin gets wider. "Huh."

"Don't let it go to your head."

"Why, was that a compliment?"

He grunts.

"So is that a yes?" He scowls, and I laugh. "I'll take that as a yes."

"Get to work, Standish."

"Rule number two—I got it, I got it…"

* * *

PHILLIP

IF ONLY SHE KNEW HOW MANY RULES I'VE BROKEN LATELY. The jacket, the crush, the nonstop talking she and I have been doing—all breaking rules I've put in place for myself.

But it's impossible not to laugh when she laughs. Or comment when she says something clever, or volley back when she teases me.

Or help when she has a question.

I'm helping her now, hand braced on her desk as I reboot her computer after it froze up, the dreaded whirling rainbow spinning round and round against the backdrop of her beloved design project, curser disappeared for good.

Control-alt-delete.

Force quit. Shut down. Restart.

I hover over her, the two of us transfixed, watching the screen come back to life after my hands contorted across her keyboard, pushing this button and that to bring the whirling to a screeching halt. Everything goes black then, seconds later— springs back to life.

Thank God.

Spencer exhales with relief when a familiar icon pops up on the monitor, the rectangular box for her password glowing. She tilts her head, glancing up at me and beaming. "Oh my goodness, thank you so much!"

"All I did was restart it." I feel my damn self blush.

We both know she could have called IT and they would have handled it, but she came to me. We both know all she had to do was restart the computer, but she didn't—she came to me.

"I could kiss you right now! I was freaking out."

Kiss me right now, kiss me right now.

I clear my throat and avert my eyes. *Do not look at her mouth, do not look at her mouth.*

That sweet, smiling mouth with those full, pink lips and straight, white teeth.

Fuck.

Like an alley rat, I scurry back to my seat. The last thing I need is an erection after getting a nose full of her musky perfume, or her seeing it.

She's not watching me, so I readjust the hardening dick in my pants.

Spencer smells so fucking good, and if she knew she was turning me on the entire time I was pressing keys on her keyboard, she's great at hiding it. Would not put it past her to purposely flip her hair so I could smell her shampoo, or lick her lips so I'd stare at her mouth.

Like a dog with my tail between my legs, I hang my head on my side of the mega-desk and pretend to work. For the first time since moving my shit into Spencer's space, I'm the one without focus. I'm the one daydreaming. I'm the one with the overactive imagination.

Or am I?

I watch her under the black rim of my glasses, the glare on the lenses from the overhead fluorescent lights masking my wandering gaze. What if she's interested, too? Then what?

Or. Perhaps she's just one of those really nice people who likes mothering people, bringing them food and small trinkets to make life easier. Like lint brushes and granola.

As much as I hate to admit it, Spencer is a sweet girl who means well, and for all the bickering we do…

It kind of turns me on, too?

Easy women are not my thing. Never have been. Bitches aren't either, but Spencer isn't really an asshole—just goofy and playful and determined as fuck.

Like me.

"Stop watching me," she tells me without looking up, tapping away like a maniac—something I have not seen her do in days.

"I'm not." I totally am.

She looks up, a lopsided grin on her face. "Stop."

"You're not the boss of me."

"You're not the boss of *me*." She's parroting our first argument from three days ago.

"Spencer, you're always bossy." *Also, stop working. I want to waste time and flirt with you and hear whatever outlandish shit you want to say.*

"If you would stop staring while I'm trying to work, we wouldn't be arguing. Take a picture—it lasts longer."

"I'm trying to take a mental picture. This is a *National Geographic* moment—you out in the wild, actually working."

"Wow Phil, those are some harsh words. Harsh." Spencer rubs her upper arm as if she's been scalded. "That burns. Burns me deep."

An eye roll and she's back to ignoring me in favor of the design layout on her screen. I want to see it, inspect it further. Get an idea of how good she is at her job.

I roll my seat away from my desk and rise. Move around the desk to stand behind her.

"What are you doing?" So suspicious this one.

"I want to see what you're working on."

"My God, please—go sit down."

"Can't. Already up."

"I cannot work with you standing over me. It's weird."

Yeah, it kind of is. Feels super intimate all of a sudden, especially when I bend to get a better look at the screen without the glare and catch a whiff of her ponytail.

Automatically, my eyes stray down the back of her neck; she has a birthmark at her nape, a cherry red one that rises up into her dark hair. I wonder if she's ever noticed, or if anyone has ever pointed it out, or if she's the type of girl who is sensitive about imperfections on her body.

Most likely? Not.

Spencer—if I've learned anything about her—would tell me to piss off if I commented on it, good or bad, because Spencer walks tall and seems to give no shits.

"If you're going to hover, you have to tell me a secret."

"Okay." I automatically agree, because I'm only half listening while openly staring at the graceful curve of her neck. "Wait —what?"

"If you're going to stand over me like you're my supervisor and watch me work, you have to pony up a secret."

"Uh—that's not even close to being a fair trade."

Her shoulders rise and fall in a shrug. "Then go sit down."

I go sit down. There are no secrets I'm willing to spill to her face, despite having a mental list of them.

1. I *am* in a secret club, Spencer, but can tell you nothing about it or I'll lose a bet.
2. Last night I dreamt of you naked. Unfortunately, Humphrey (who sleeps at the foot of the bed) was chasing squirrels in between snoring and woke me up mid-dream—but I confess you were not wearing clothes, and I woke up with a raging hard-on this morning. Thanks to you.
3. Speaking of raging hard-ons: once, in high school, I passed out naked in the locker room while taking a shower, and the guys started a rumor that I have a micro-penis.
4. I do not, in fact, have a tiny dick.
5. Some of the assholes from high school still call me Tiny.
6. Occasionally my sister does, too.

We're quiet for a while; I manage to focus my concentration

on a development project. Schedule a meeting for the morning so I won't have to rush in—so I won't have to sit and covertly gawk at Spencer like a creep.

God, I'm a pervert.

The day drags on and I find myself watching the clock.

Three o'clock and we haven't spoken in an hour. Spencer ordered us lunch at noon, leaving only to grab the delivery from the lobby, returning with two brown paper bags.

She plunked one on my desk, out of my way, fumes wafting to my nose and making my stomach groan. I polished off a hot roast beef sandwich in record time, and the baked beans and slaw that came with it.

For a girl who likes to boss me around, she sure knows how to spoil me.

Secret number 7: I'm going to miss her after tomorrow.

Returning to my own office is going to suck balls come Monday. Granted, it will have nice, new carpet—but I'd rather have chatty, giving Spencer.

11

SPENCER

It's not often I stay in the office working late—I usually don't have to—but I'm on a roll with this design, and I'm afraid if I move from this desk, I'll lose momentum.

So here I am, moving my mouse around its pad, mind wandering as I click away and create.

I had today and tomorrow with Phillip, and I'm already dreading the empty space on the other side of my desk. How lonely I'll probably feel now that I've gotten used to his presence, how quiet the room will be without him.

Like right now. Eerily quiet.

Almost everyone has gone home except the owner of the company, the chief financial officer, and the secretary the owner is banging. Er—the one he's in a relationship with? Cough, cough.

Until six o'clock, I could hear the carpenters on the south side hammering or pulling up carpet or whatever it is they're doing over there (I haven't checked). Then slowly, little by little, those sounds faded, and the only company I'm keeping is the honking cars and the train outside my office window.

A few lights have been left on, but otherwise, only a few offices are lit.

Numerous times, I've thought about music, about playing it low for background noise—company. But I started cranking away without it and I don't want to jinx myself, so I work, head bent in the silence.

The logo I'm designing for an industrial development outside the city is modern and sleek, a cool mix of silver and blue. I've added several buildings but no—

"Hey! What are you still doing here?"

"Holy shit!" I about crap myself, knocking over a container of pens and markers with my flailing arms. "You scared me half to death!"

Phillip is standing in the doorway, ever-present laptop bag slung over his shoulder, black pea coat buttoned to the throat, baseball cap thrown on his head.

Oh Jesus, he looks so cute.

And thank God he's not my boss. If I said *Holy shit you scared me* to the owner or CFO of the company, I would die from mortification.

"Sorry. I didn't mean to scare you." His grin says otherwise.

"No, it's fine. Only a mild heart attack." I press my hand to my heart, feeling it race. "Whew! No biggie."

"I think I'm just as surprised to see you here as you are me." He steps inside, cheeks flushed from the cold weather, tips of his ears bright red.

"I felt inspired so I kept at it. What are *you* doing here?"

"I forgot my power cord." He leans down and unplugs it from the wall. "I was all the way home before I realized it and the dog chewed up my spare." He stands with the cord in his clenched hand, the black plastic hanging like a snake in his grip. "I guess I'll just…"

He nods toward the door, intending to leave. Hesitates.

I smile, nervously running a hand down the length of my ponytail.

Giggle.

Oh Lord…

"Do you want some company?" His man bag is halfway down his arm, resting on the chair.

"No, no—you go ahead home. I only have about an hour left."

The last time I checked, it was already past seven, but this design is still fresh in my mind, requiring more attention. If I stay on track, I can complete this project ahead of schedule, and wouldn't that be a first?!

"Are you sure? I don't mind." The laptop bag is on the floor now, Phillip unbuttoning his coat, one toggle at a time. He plops down in his chair, palming his phone. "What should we eat? Want anything to drink? Coffee, tea?"

"You're going to feed me?"

"I have to return the favor, don't I?"

"No." I blush. Dammit, I'm blushing. I've blushed so many times in the past few days I've lost count. I feel like a high school kid again, but it feels good. "But if you're ordering food, I wouldn't kick you out of bed."

He looks up then, expression frozen.

"Shit. I didn't mean—I mean, it's... I say that all the time. It's an expression."

Phillip gulps, tapping on his phone. "I know. It just caught me off guard."

"Yeah, I can't imagine you're a saint—I'm sure some pretty colorful language comes out of your mouth."

Your beautiful, full mouth.

To his credit, he doesn't deny it. Instead, he laughs. "I can throw down an F bomb when necessary."

My brows arch. "When is it necessary to use the word fuck in a sentence?"

"Did you just swear at me?"

"Not at you—to you." I smile innocently, pleased by the shocked expression on his face. Good. I like surprising people; no doubt he's misjudged me a few times this week. Probably as a girl who takes nothing seriously, or one who has a shitty work ethic.

Which…sometimes I do, yeah—sue me.

Just don't fire me, ha.

"I don't know how to feel about you saying the word fuck. It's weird."

"Why? Because I'm so sweet?"

Phillip regards me, choosing his words. "Kind of."

What? WHAT? Is he being serious right now? He cannot casually call me *sweet* like that!

"Oh? You think I'm sweet kind of?" I'm shamelessly fishing for compliments and I don't care.

"I see glimpses of it."

"What else?" I force my eyes to the computer monitor so I appear as casual as possible, eagerly anticipating his response.

"Uh…um. Hmm."

He has to think about it? Well, shit. That's not promising.

I wait.

"You're goofy."

Goofy? That's not cute or adorable. That's…goofy.

I don't reply because I'm not happy with that description of myself. I purse my lips.

Phillip laughs. "Okay sourpuss, I wasn't insulting you." He looks down at his phone. "Medium tea or small?"

I sniff indignantly. "Medium."

From beneath my lashes, I see him hiding a grin in the collar of his dress shirt. He taps a few more times and nods, satisfied, setting the phone on the surface of his desk. "Dinner will be here in less than forty-five if we're lucky."

"Thanks. I am getting hungry, and there's nothing but carbs in the breakroom—I've had my fill for the day."

"You can stop pouting. I wasn't done listing off all your adorable qualities."

Adorable? That's more like it. I perk up, straightening my back a bit.

"Sweet, most days. Giving—in a motherly way." He pauses, thoughtful. "You're funny and…"

And?

And!

I lean forward, trying not to come off as desperate for his praise, but I'm desperate for his praise. Even if he thinks I'm giving in a *motherly* way. *Relax, Spencer—he didn't call you matronly. He said motherly—not the same thing. Chill out.*

"I've, um…watched how you interact with people in the office, and everyone loves you."

Aw, they do? "They do?" This is news to me; I assumed most people find me exasperating.

"Yeah, they do. People gravitate toward someone outgoing. I've noticed when you go out into the common area, at least one person comes out of their office to talk with you."

I consider this new information. Come to think of it, he's right—if I'm standing around near the cubicles, inevitably, one of my co-workers will come out of their office to chat. I'm shocked Phillip has noticed. I'm flattered, and…

Does this mean he watches me when I'm not looking? When I walk out of this office, do his eyes follow me?

I store this news away in my brain, mentally doing somersaults and cartwheels but schooling my expression.

"Well. Other than you barfing in his trash can, I happen to know for a fact that Paul wants to be your friend."

Phillip gawks. Then blinks. "He does *not*."

I nod, holding up two fingers—scout's honor. "He does. And I don't mean in a 'he wants to date you' kind of a way, because I think he has a boyfriend, but he wants to hang out with you. Something about a dog park and your Basset Hound?"

"No shit?"

"No shit."

* * *

PHILLIP

"...AND THEN, MY OLDER BROTHER AND SISTER HAD TO explain to me that being called Tuna Fish at school was not cool."

"Wait—tell me again why the hell you wanted to be called Tuna Fish?" I stab a piece of ninja roll sushi with a chopstick and shove it in my mouth whole, eel sauce catching on the corner of my mouth.

Since the sushi takeout arrived, we haven't done shit as far as actually working, talking instead. How we found ourselves seated on the floor, beside the desks, backs against the wall, I do not know.

But we're down here, laughing and telling stories, cartons of food scattered.

"I was in fourth grade, and a few days a week I would wear this dolphin shirt. My mom had to constantly wash it and it faded pretty quick, but I loved it. I was on a save the dolphins kick, you know? Total animal freak. Once at a water park, I swam around pretending to be a trout. I also wanted to save the wolves."

Oh boy.

Spencer goes on. "So I wore the shit out of this shirt, and one of my little buddies starts calling me Tuna Fish. I think this is great, right? Running around the playground being called Tuna Fish." We both laugh. "I mean, what the heck did I know? I was ten, and everyone else at school was using nicknames, and since I actually did love tuna, I went home and made the announcement to my family."

Dear God.

"*Yeah*, I can see by the appalled expression on your face you're having the same reaction my mother did." Spencer is spooning up egg-drop soup and blowing it off to cool it. "Except Mom was too shook to tell me calling her preteen daughter

Tuna Fish wasn't going to happen. She bribed my older brother and sister with gift cards to the ski hill to break the bad news."

"What did they say?"

"They said, '*Spencer, you stupid idiot, don't let them call you Tuna Fish.*' I was so confused. Then my sister goes, '*It means fish, but it's also…kind of like saying your crotch smells. Do you want people to think your crotch smells?*'"

I sputter on my tea. "Your sister said that?"

"Brutal, those two." She's shaking her head at the memory, a smile playing on her lips. "I mean—they did me a favor by telling me the truth, so I went to school the next day and told everyone to stop calling me Tuna Fish, and I stopped wearing that T-shirt. Can you imagine? That name would have followed me through high school." Her head shakes at the mere thought and she shivers. "Nightmare."

I agree. "I wouldn't have wanted to ask a girl called Tuna Fish to prom."

A one-shoulder shrug. "I never went to prom anyway."

"You didn't?" The news surprises me; if Spencer was half as cute as a teenager as she is now, I can't believe boys weren't beating down her door.

"Nah, I scared most guys away." She pops a slice of ginger onto her tongue and chews. Swallows. "Asking out an outspoken female teenager when you're seventeen is intimidating. Guys always liked to date giggly, feminine girls, and I was too…"

"Wild?"

"No."

"*Crazy?*"

"No—oh my God, Phillip, would you let me finish?"

"Sure." But I don't need her to; I know how young guys are when it comes to strong, independent girls. How men react to strong, independent women—I know exactly what Spencer is going to tell me.

"I scared them off because I said what was on my mind." She's digging into the soup again, insatiable. "Everyone says what they want is someone who doesn't play games, but in reality, that's not what they want at all. Men can't handle it."

"You can't stereotype us all."

She glances up, spoon poised to hit her lips. "Are you saying that's what you want? Someone who tells it like it is?"

"If I were dating—*if*—then yeah, that's what I'd want." But she's right. Last week I might have felt different, but now that I've met Spencer, I think someone like her would be good for me. Unlike the girls in the past, the ones who agreed with everything I said. The ones who giggled and laughed, even when I wasn't trying to be funny. Who wanted to be taken care of so they wouldn't have to work.

Which is fine; to each their own.

But admit it. Don't lie.

Spencer looks skeptical but doesn't press for more information. Instead, she says, "What about you? What's a secret about something embarrassing? I told you mine."

"That was from fourth grade—hardly the same. That story was more adorable than humiliating."

She considers this. "I suppose. But I still want to hear what you have to say."

"Okay, give me a minute." While I'm racking my brain, I continue shoving sushi into my gullet. The impromptu picnic has satisfied my appetite. I don't know *what* I was craving, but this? This moment?

I want more of it.

Three more pieces of ninja roll and I wipe my hands on the napkin folded across my lap, licking my lips. Stretch my legs in front of me and grin. "Okay, I thought of something. It's not nearly as good as you getting your period at school, but I did once get a boner during math class." I can feel the blush over my entire body, and curse myself for saying the word boner. Regret it instantly. "On second thought, never mind."

"Oh come on!" Spencer whines. "You have to tell me about your surprise boner!"

"First of all, don't call it a surprise boner." I laugh, folding my arms. "Secondly, just forget it. I shouldn't have mentioned it."

"Lame." She gives me a thumbs down, and a pouty lower lip.

"When I was a kid," I begin slowly. "My mom would put me in the worst fucking clothes, and they were always a few sizes too big so I could grow into them." She did it to my sister, too. "For picture day one year—can't remember what grade, maybe second—she made me wear this plaid shirt and khakis."

"Aww."

"No, not aww. It was embarrassing. I was seven and looked like a tiny nerd—what self-respecting dude wants to wear plaid and khakis on picture day? I wanted to wear my Captain America T-shirt and mesh track pants."

"Uh-huh, says the guy with a surprise boner." She's eating and listening attentively, sprawled out next to me in what she called her "Thursday dressy jeans" and a light lavender sweater. It looks soft and touchable.

Er.

Yeah.

Focus, Phillip.

"So I'm in this outfit, and my mom insists on taking a picture before I leave, and since I'm mad about it, I slouch and make the dumbest face. When she developed the film, I found the picture and tore it up, but she found it and dug it out of the trash and taped it back together."

"That's actually adorable that you'd do that, all mad and angry."

"There's more," I explain. "The picture gets pinned to the pegboard, all taped up. When I was in college I was dating this one girl and she had a photography class, so she took the photo and repaired it, or whatever it is photographers do to fix pictures —you couldn't even tell I'd torn it up."

"That was nice of her!"

"Yeah." My head is resting against the wall and I look up at the ceiling, studying the lights and the ceiling tiles. "I have an older sister, Lisbeth. She's an asshole, thinks everything is a big joke. One weekend she was home, she took a picture of the picture on her phone because my mom still has the damn thing on the pegboard, even to this day, and every once in a while, Lisbeth will superimpose what everyone calls 'Little Angry Phillip' onto different pictures of me. Like the family photo from my cousin's wedding—little angry me is in the background looking like a tiny serial killer."

"Can I see? You must have it saved on your phone."

I do, because Lisbeth sends so goddamn many of them in the family group texts. Me at Comic-Con with Little Angry Phillip. Me and my buddies at a bachelor party with Little Angry Phillip. Christmas pictures. Christenings. Vacations.

Like when does she have time for all that dumb shit?

I thumb through my gallery, selfies and photographs of construction sites whizzing by as my finger nudges the feed along, Spencer scooting closer so she can peek. Shoulder brushing mine. Knees touching.

My body reacts.

Damn—it's either been too long since I've had sex, or I'm ridiculously attracted to her. Or both.

I clear my throat, not sure what else to do. Point to a photoshopped picture of myself with my younger self that my sister created on her laptop as a joke. "See?"

Spencer leans farther over, breasts brushing my arm. "Dude, that is hilarious! I love your sister."

"Don't. She's a monster."

"Oh come on, she can't be all that bad if one of her favorite hobbies is to torture you via humiliation."

True. She does like doing that. "Isn't that also one of your favorite hobbies?"

Spencer nods. "That and knitting."

My brows go up and I turn my head to look at her. "You knit?"

"No, but I want to knit a poncho." She sighs deeply into her spoonful of wonton soup. "I took a knitting class once and lasted exactly one hour—it's just not the sport for me."

"Sport?"

"I'm not athletic, and it takes hand-eye coordination."

"You're such a weirdo."

"Aww." She lays her head on my shoulder as she says it. Classic chick move. "You're the sweetest. I love it when you compliment me."

"That wasn't—" I stop myself short because in reality, calling her a weirdo was kind of a compliment. "You're certainly not like anyone I've ever met."

Spencer lets out another flattered "Aww" and smirks. "Stop, you're making me blush. I'm overcome." She pauses. "Even though I have no idea what you mean by that."

I do.

I mean: Spencer is funny and sassy wrapped up in one. Sweet and giving. Kind to everyone (everyone but me, ha). Generous with her time (and food), always willing to answer questions around the office. Willing to stand and listen to our co-workers drone on and on about themselves or their free time, boasting about their dating lives or something they did over the weekend.

Spencer is not boastful or spoiled or catty. She's not stuck-up or selfish.

I don't say any of this out loud.

Another light in the office goes dark.

She lifts her head and sits up straighter. "What time is it?"

We lost track of it a while ago.

I tap my phone. "Shit, it's almost nine."

"Almost nine? Dang! I've never stayed this late." She stretches, her elbow brushing my side, ponytail swishing.

It kicks up the scent of her shampoo, and I sneak a whiff.

"You really have to stop sniffing me—it's weird."

"I…" Do I bother denying it? I decide no. Change the

subject. "I've been gone forever—I have to let the dog out, and play with him," I groan. "He's going to be a maniac."

We gather our dinner, stacking cartons on the desks, cups and bowls.

"Poor guy."

And poor me—I'm going to be up all damn night with him. Humphrey might be low-hanging fruit, aka low to the ground and built like a Tonka Truck, but he has energy to spare, especially when he's been home sleeping all day.

I hadn't planned on being at the office so long, and now little dude is going to be stir crazy, not to mention he's going to have to piss, if he hasn't peed in the house already.

Shit.

Peed or shit.

That would be a crappy ending to an awesome day, pun intended.

"Thanks again for dinner, Phillip."

Goddamn if I don't love the way she says my name. Casually, with a hint of…something I can't put my finger on. A flirty little subtext I can't describe.

Thanks again for dinner, *Phil*-lip.

"And thank you for keeping me company." Spencer hesitates, unsure. "It was…nice."

There's that word again.

Nice.

"How are you getting home?" I ask, tossing the cartons in the garbage can then placing it in the hallway.

Her ponytail swishes. "The train? I live about ten blocks away. Near Station Twelve."

Huh. I'm near Station Twelve, too. "I'm about ten blocks." Nine to be exact, but close enough. "Share a ride? It's late—let's not take the train. Plus it'll be quicker, and I've gotta bust it home."

Also, I want to spend more time with her.

Sue me.

"Sure, we could share a ride." I swear she's blushing again. "Want me to..." She wiggles her phone in the air.

I hold mine up and flash the already active ride app. "I got it."

Yup, she's definitely blushing.

12

SPENCER

Our ride is a tiny, black hybrid with room enough for three, and when it pulls up to the curb outside our glossy high-rise of an office building, Phillip lunges forward to get the door. Pulls it open and gestures.

"Ladies first."

I smile as I scoot past him, grateful he isn't the type to sit in front with the driver—I want his attention. I don't want him sitting in the passenger seat making small talk with the guy driving.

Phillip's laptop bag divides the back seat and he confirms our two locations, glancing at me. "You're on Brady?"

I nod. "Yes."

"I'm on Central." Just two blocks over—in city terms, that's as good as being next door.

"Who knew?" My whole body glows with an unexplained happiness I know I shouldn't be feeling—this is not a date. He is not my boyfriend. He does not like me.

We work together.

But.

The chemistry…

I know the ride won't last long; I've done it enough times—

twenty minutes tops, and that's during rush-hour traffic. It's after nine right now, so it's practically a ghost town on these side streets our driver begins navigating through, passing townhouses and apartments.

I'm in an apartment, above a townhouse, four stories up. Real talk: I live in an attic. Real talk: the pigeons and occasional dove on my window ledges drive me freaking insane, especially when they shit all over, leaving things a mess. I hate seeing the bird turd as much as I loathe being woken up at the butt crack of dawn on a day I can sleep in.

Damn birds.

In companionable silence, we weave up and down streets. Pretty, tree-lined streets with families tucked away inside.

Our car hangs a right near my neighborhood. Slows.

"My place is up here on the left." Phillip leans forward to explain. "The one with the hedges and black fence."

Well la-di-da—isn't he fancy.

In reality, I'm shocked by this new development. Phillip is younger than I am; the fact that he is more established domestically chafes a little as we pull up to his house.

It's a lovely brownstone; had to have cost a bundle. I wonder where he got the money, speculating that it must have been an inheritance. Or risky investment that paid off.

Phillip is twenty-eight—how does he own a house in the city?

"I love it," I say, leaning forward so I can gaze out the window at the brick building with its tidy hedgerow and shiny, decorative wrought iron fence. "Do you have the entire place?"

"Yeah." He doesn't explain further, just hefts his man purse bag to his lap. Phillip gazes out the window, too. "God, the dog must be losing his mind." He glances at me. "I hope he doesn't start peeing when I walk through the door."

"Nervous pee-er?" I ask.

Phillip confirms this with a laugh.

"Me too," I tell him, just to get a reaction. "But I bet he's adorable. I've never actually met a Basset Hound in real life—only seen them in the movies."

He laughs again, gesturing toward the house. "Do you want to meet one now? I mean, real quick? I have to walk him a bit, so maybe…"

Is he offering to walk me the rest of the way home?

"…he and I can walk you the rest of the way home. You said it's only a block over?"

"Two." I nervously futz with my ponytail.

"That's kind of perfect. You want to come up while I grab him?"

Um—do I? Hell yes. Not only do I want to see his dog and spend more time with him, I'm dying to see the inside of his brownstone.

I gather up my stuff: purse, laptop—check, check. Give the seat and floor around me a once-over to be sure neither of us are forgetting anything.

Phillip waits, hand on the doorframe as I shimmy my way across the pleather seat and climb out, eyes scanning the façade of his house. It's three stories high with red brick, white trim, and a black door.

Wow.

I'm impressed.

Do not ask where he got the money for this place, do not ask where he got the money for this place… It's rude. Don't.

"Did you win the lottery?" I blurt out.

Dammit Spencer, what did I just get done telling you? Ugh, have some class.

Phillip takes it in stride, laughing. "Right?" Fumbles with a set of keys for the deadbolt, enters four digits into the keypad below it. "I inherited it when my grandmother died. They had a few places around the city as investments, this was one of them. I got one, my sister got one—she sold hers because she doesn't live here and it didn't make sense paying all those property taxes."

This makes so much more sense than him buying it.

"I've been renovating for the past two years." He pushes the front door open, revealing a black and white tiled entry hall with coat hooks to the right and a shoe rack to the left.

Clean. Tidy.

So, so pretty.

Another set of door codes and he is motioning for me to enter the foyer, a staircase running up the length of the right wall. Flips on three light switches. Tosses his keys in a bowl, on a table, next to the second door.

Phillip purses his lips and lets out a low whistle.

I hear the hoofbeats of a stampeding horse galloping toward the foyer. Hear the panting energy. The beast crashes into something I cannot see, followed by another crash, more stampeding.

"Oh Jesus," Phillip says. "Brace yourself."

"Shit, now I'm scared."

"He's loud, but squat. You'll see."

13

PHILLIP

Spencer is here. In my house.

Which shouldn't be a big deal since I've obviously had women at my place before. And this isn't a date by any stretch of the imagination. We shared a car ride home—that is it.

So why is my fucking heart racing? Why are my damn palms sweating? I could barely insert the key into my deadbolt, and I almost forgot the code to get into the house.

"Oh Jesus." I breathe out a sigh, listening as Humphrey comes barreling through the house as fast as his short legs can carry him, smashing into what can only be the trophy table I have in my home office—a place he loves sleeping when I'm gone. "Brace yourself."

"Shit, now I'm scared." Spencer grins good-naturedly.

"He's loud, but squat." I try to explain, as if it wasn't obvious he's loud. You'd have to be deaf not to hear the short bastard roaring through the house. "You'll see."

The panting gets noisier; I can practically hear the drool flying from his tongue and onto my hardwood floors, make a mental note to wipe them down when we get back from our walk.

1. Pick up whatever he broke.
2. Wipe up spit and drool.
3. Jerk off before bed.

God, it's been forever since I've stroked my dick, and now that I have inspiration, I'm not going to squander it...

The dog is careening around the corner, skidding while I cringe, his claws digging into the recently refurbished floors.

He rounds the corner, drool flying, ears flapping.

Goddamn he's a sight.

Spencer gasps when she lays eyes on him.

Goes down on bended knee to accept his attack. "Hello handsome boy! How are you?!"

He smashes into her unceremoniously, knocking her back onto her ass. Uses the opportunity to climb on top and lick her face.

"Off!" I shout. "Humphrey, off!"

Humphrey does not listen.

"Grab my hand," I instruct as Spencer lies on my floor laughing, purse and laptop bag strewn around her. Damn dog.

I reach down and offer my palm, pull her to her feet.

Spencer brushes off her knees and ass, bemused, now covered in dog hair. She squats again, this time not so far down as to allow herself to be victimized.

"Aw, look at you!" She coos in a baby voice reserved for pooches. "Look how handsome you are, what a pretty boy!" She casts a glance up at me with her own set of puppy dog eyes while the dog basks in her petting and praise, his eyes sliding halfway shut at the attention. "What's his name again?"

"Humphrey."

"What?" She stops stroking the dog long enough to scrunch up her pretty features. "You named your dog *Humpy?*"

"No—Humphrey, with a P-H. Why the hell would I name my dog Humpy?"

Is she out of her mind? Who would do that?

"'Cause you're a guy? And guys do stupid shit like that?" It's not the first time I've heard her swear, but I haven't gotten used to the sound of profanity coming from her lips.

"Spencer, I must have said his name twenty times now."

"Maybe I just wanted to hear you say Humpy."

Jezebel, this one. *She is no good for me.*

The dog likes it too, because he chooses that moment to stick his nose in her crotch.

Spencer gasps. "Oh Jesus!" Moves his face with her hands and laughs but backs away, tilting her body away from the dog's probing nostrils.

"He has to go out—I'm surprised he hasn't peed on us." I shoot the dog a look. "Okay buddy, go get your leash."

We wait.

"He can fetch his own leash? Wow!" Spencer is suitably impressed.

"Humphrey—get your leash! Go get it!"

He does not go get it.

"I'll be right back. It's hanging in the kitchen." I spare a glare for the disobedient dog. "Stay."

Obviously he stays.

As if he's going anywhere—his new love is hitting all his favorite spots with her pink polished nails: behind his ears and along his neck, beneath his collar.

Is it possible I'm jealous of the dog?

Yes.

I retrieve the leash, attempting to calm the dog so I can snap it to his collar. He's so excited he's bouncing on his back legs, a hoppy little jig of anticipation. *Hold still, dude,* I silently plead, not wanting to lose my patience in front of Spencer.

Humphrey continues hopping, making it damn near impossible to clasp the silver buckle to his neck. When I finally secure it, I stand, making sure Spencer has all her stuff before we head out.

"Ready?" I give her a once-over: purse, computer bag.

"Ready when you are."

Everything is great for the first few steps; everyone stays in line, the evening brisk but not unbearably cold. It's not far to the end of the block, and I consider how close she and I are in proximity.

Right beneath my nose.

Humphrey sniffs the sidewalk as he ambles on. Finds a spot and pees.

Great. "Good dog."

He loves the praise.

"You said you've been remodeling for the past two years— what have you done with your place?"

My brain mentally ticks off the list of renovations I've done to my house. "It wasn't in bad shape. Luckily most of it was original, and you know how uncommon that is. New owners and renters love nothing more than ripping out cool shit and replacing it with crap."

Spencer nods like she knows what I'm talking about, so I go on.

"Let's see…I started with the floors. Stripped them myself before I moved in and stained them the dark color. Which, in retrospect, I regret—that dark stain shows everything."

I shoot a pointed look at the culprit sauntering along in front of me.

"Floors. New fixtures in the kitchen and all the bathrooms— took me months to find the right ones because I didn't want anything modern. Uh…I had to replace a few windows that had lead or were rotted. Bathroom tile. Tile in the entry. Last spring, I did the landscaping out front and painted the fence."

"By yourself?"

"Not all of it. I have a few buddies who are handy with a hammer." Sort of. Brooks Bennett is semi-useful when it comes to do-it-yourself home improvement. Blaine? Not so much, but they showed up when I needed them, and that counts for something.

"The friends you were with at The Basement?" she questions.

"Yeah."

"Have you been friends with them long?"

"Since high school."

"That's so great—I have a few friends like that. I met Miranda in college, and I consider her my best friend even if she's a monster most of the time."

I laugh. "How is she a monster? I thought Humphrey was the only one of those around." The dog glances up, regarding me after hearing his name.

"She's loud and really outgoing, so when we're in public…" Her voice trails off. "I'm not going to approach a group of guys and insert myself into the conversation like she will."

"You? Shy?"

"I didn't say shy—I'm just not bold like that."

I'm glad to learn this about her. Miranda seemed fun, but her personality would wear on me after a while if I had to be friends with her.

The kind of girl who threatens to cut a dude's nuts off if he hurts her best friend.

That's the kind of girl Miranda is: loyal and scary.

"You three looked pretty comfortable at that bar. Do you go there often?"

"It's our spot."

"Looked like it." She pauses, and the sound of leaves rustling fills the air. "For your club meetings?"

"Yes," I say absentmindedly. "Shit—no."

Spencer laughs again. "Too late. Busted!"

Fuck.

"So that's the deal with the jackets. You have a club? Hmm," she hums. "Can I guess what kind?"

"No!" I nearly shout, losing control of the situation. Between Spencer and the dog, my nerves are buzzing. Hormones and testosterone raging. "I mean—no. I wouldn't be able to tell you even if you guessed, so—leave it alone." Then, feeling guilty for being harsh, I add, "I'm not trying to be a dick, but we have rules."

Shit. I probably shouldn't have said that either.

No matter—Spencer is never going to bump into Blaine and Brooks again. Hopefully. Unless, of course, she comes back to The Basement, though she didn't look at all comfortable there, not like her friend Miranda did.

"You love your rules, don't you?"

Not really. They just happen. "Sure."

A small bob of understanding. "I get it. I was in a sorority in college."

"It's not like a sorority," I mutter.

"Fraternity."

"It's not—we're not a secret society," I lie. "Our rules are pretty stupid, just for fun."

"Secret rules you can't talk about." Her eyes are rolling. "Sounds like a secret society, but what do I know?"

More than you think, I want to confess.

1. You know we wear matching smoking jackets to our meetings.
2. You know where our meetings are held.
3. You know who the members are.
4. You know we have rules.
5. You saw me freak out when you tried my jacket on, so you know letting you wear it is not allowed.
6. You know we have a secret club.

"It's not one of those dumb clubs where everyone vows to stay single, is it?" She laughs loudly, snorting. "That would be the most idiotic thing I've ever heard of in my entire life."

Spencer is kidding around. She has no idea how close to home she's hitting, and the pit in my stomach drops.

I feel physically ill.

Trip on a crack in the concrete at the same time Humphrey

stops in the middle of the sidewalk, and we stroll past him until the leash goes taut.

He isn't moving.

Not a good sign, but he takes the heat off of me and Spencer's conspiracy theories. *One point awarded to Humphrey for saving my ass.*

"What's he doing?" Spencer wonders, cocking her head in Humphrey's direction.

"He's being stubborn."

"Why?"

"Because that is what he does, which is why I'm late for work almost every day." I stand, engaged in a battle of wills with the dog, a dog who chooses the world's most inopportune moments to act like an asshole.

"We've gone a block and a half—I can see my place." Spencer points down the street. "I'm there, in the middle. The dark gray townhouse."

If only we can make it that far without me having to—

"Does he want you to…" Spencer's head tilts farther in thought. "It seems like he wants you to carry him."

Yes, that's *exactly* what the fucker wants. Except I'm not giving in so soon—this late-night deadlock is bullshit, and if I have to carry him on the way back, I'm going to be seriously pissed.

"How long is he going to stand there like that?" Under the glow of the streetlamp overhead, I can see her trying not to laugh.

I wouldn't blame her one bit; this is stupid.

"He'll stand there like that until he decides to lie down." It will be one or the other. "It's a showdown. We have them a few times a week, usually in the morning."

"Does he always want to be carried?"

"Um, no." He just wants attention, and if you would stop petting him, maybe he would walk like a normal dog. One who doesn't insist on staying put, refusing to walk another step farther until I bend down and scoop him up.

Jesus Christ he's heavier than a giant bag of dog food.

"What a goofy dog!" Spencer exclaims.

"Goofy is not how I would describe him," I pant, already out of breath. Thank God her place is right freaking there. In a few minutes I'll be able to put the dog down. "Last week he pretended to have a limp."

"He did not!"

"Yup. He dragged his hind quarters down the sidewalk like his back leg was broken, like a stray in a tourist town." Goofy does not begin to describe this dog.

Humphrey luxuriates in having my arms wrapped around him, head held high as if he is front and center in a parade, one starring him, with people there to view him and only him.

Such a showboating spectacle.

He takes the opportunity to let out a howl of pleasure, alerting anyone within earshot of his presence.

"Shh, *no*," I tell him sternly. "Do you want me to put you down?"

He stops bleating like the town crier.

"That dog is…really something else." Spencer giggles. "I would offer to babysit for him if you ever go out of town, but honestly, I don't know if I'd be able to handle it."

"Believe me, we've gone through a whole roster of babysitters. There is only one person he listens to, and it isn't me. Her name is Stacy and she's eighteen. She must smell like bacon and chicken cutlets, because he adores her and listens to everything she says."

"Why do you sound so annoyed?"

"Because it annoys me that he doesn't give a shit about anything I say."

"Does he know you're the boss? You're the leader of his pack."

I shoot her an irritated look. "You think I haven't taken him to obedience classes? Literally nothing works for this dog. He does. Not. Give. A. Shit. I mean, look at him!" I try to hoist the dog higher to illustrate my point, but he's overweight and I'm afraid I'll drop him.

"Maybe if you didn't pick him up every time he wanted to be picked up..." Spencer starts.

I silence her with my narrowed stare, the dog and I now panting in unison.

Spencer puts up her hands in mock retreat. "Okay, okay, I'm only saying. Sorry." Nothing can hide the grin on her pretty face. "He does look like a chunky handful. Literally."

Ha fucking ha. But he is. "It feels like he weighs a million pounds."

"You must be strong though if you can carry all that weight so many blocks," Spencer demurs, bowing her head and burying her face in the collar of her shirt, flirting.

That's what she's doing, isn't it? Flirting? Shit. It's been so long since a woman has been coy with me, I barely know what it looks like anymore.

I set the dog down, much to his ire. He grunts unhappily but forgets to be stubborn when he discovers a new bush to sniff and explore.

Good, he's distracted.

Gripping his lead, I stuff my hands in my pockets as Spencer hesitates on the steps up to her door.

"Is this whole place yours?" I ask, curious.

"No, it's actually an apartment. I'm the top."

The top.

My mind goes into the gutter, picturing her on top. *Of me.*

"It's cute," she says. "Expensive, but cute."

"Bet it's no fun when you have groceries." I know I don't enjoy having to haul shit in, and my kitchen is on the first floor of my brownstone, not up three stories of narrow stairs.

"It's not fun, even when I don't have groceries. Moving in was terrible. Luckily it came half furnished—granted, the couch is shitty. I've only fallen through it once, though, so that's a plus."

Why are we standing here, making idle chitchat? It's not exactly warm and toasty outside, and my hands are getting cold even though they're stuffed in my pockets. Spencer is rambling about her apartment, the fact that she couldn't move a new sofa in unless it went through a window. She rambles about…birds?

She's adorable, and I consider what I would do if we had been drinking tonight, what I would do if I had liquid courage. Would I lean in to kiss her?

Whoa, Phillip, way to get ahead of yourself. Calm down, boy, you are not putting your lips on her—not tonight.

Humphrey is the only lucky bastard who will have that honor.

Nonetheless, my eyes stray to her mouth as she speaks, the glossy lipstick or lip balm or whatever that is that's shiny as a spotlight and drawing my eyes there. They move, bottom lip plump, her teeth occasionally pulling on it.

Is she nervous? She doesn't look nervous…

Not Spencer. Of the two of us, she's the one who is always in control. Calm, cute, collected.

The dog whines (nothing new there), and she glances down, face transformed by her smile. Spencer squats, showering Humphrey with attention.

"What, are you bored? Huh? Are we boring you with all our talk?" She pets and scratches brown fur. "Thank you for walking me home, Humphrey. Be a good boy and walk home without having to be carried, yes, be a good boy. Such a good boy," she croons. "Pretty pretty puppy."

He hasn't been a puppy in three years, having just turned five. I chuckle at the thought of what a goddamn asshole he was as a pup.

When she rises, her hand grips the wrought iron stair rail; it's rusted and could use a good sandblasting. Definitely needs a coat of paint.

I stare at Spencer's fingers so long she wiggles them so I'll lift my gaze. She takes a step back, up the stairs. One. Then another. I'm compelled to do the same. Something about not seeing her all the way to the door feels ungentlemanly—or that's what I'll tell myself in the morning—so I follow all the way to the top, Humphrey lagging behind, leash slack between us, dragging on the ground.

"You didn't have to ride home with me, or walk me here, for that matter," Spencer says, turning at the top once she reaches the door.

"It wasn't a big deal. Maybe we should start carpooling every day." Ha ha. I'm only partially joking, and now that I've said the words out loud, the idea of it takes root in my brain, sprouting. Shit. I should not be making plans to spend more time with her —nothing good would come of it. She would get too attached and I'd have to let her down easy.

I should be pushing her away.

Spencer's brows go up, disbelieving. "Did you just suggest we ride to work together?"

"No."

"Yes you did." She pats me on the arm. "Aww, that was sweet. You like me."

I do fucking like her.

Her hand on my bicep blazes through my wool coat and I glance down at it, those long fingers. The pink nails.

"What's that look for?" She wants to know, removing her hand.

"What look?"

"You look strange all of a sudden, like…"

I think she's going to tell me I look distant. Or confused. Or tired.

"…you have to shit yourself." Pretty Spencer with the potty mouth laughs. "Constipated."

Gee. Thanks.

"Don't make that face—I'm only teasing." She giggles again,

the sound filling the night. "Don't you like being teased, Phillip?"

Jesus, the tone of her voice. I doubt she's intentionally trying to sound sexy, but she does, and it's doing shit to the dick in my pants.

I clear my throat.

She clears hers. "So. Anyway. Thanks for bringing me home."

"No problem."

"You don't actually want to carpool in the morning, do you?"

"Maybe not tomorrow. I have a thing."

A thing? Way to think quick on your feet, Phillip—it doesn't sound at all like you're backpedaling.

"It's fine, I get it." She lets me off the hook. "And it's our last day together! We should celebrate."

Celebrate something I'm not looking forward to? I don't think so.

"What?"

"Huh?"

"You just said, *Celebrate something I'm not looking forward to?*"

"I said that out loud?" Shit, I'm losing my touch.

"Yes, you said that out loud. Wow, Phillip, I knew you liked me, but I didn't think you *liked me* liked me."

"Don't get ahead of yourself," I joke even as the knot in my stomach tightens.

"I won't lord it over you. Mostly because I'm not going to see you after tomorrow." Her smile goes from jovial to a bit morose. "Anyway. You should get that beast of a mutt home so you're not up all night hanging out with him."

We both look down at Humphrey. He's sitting on the concrete stoop watching the street. Content.

"He'll be exhausted by the time we get to my place."

"Yeah right—you're going to have to carry him."

Negative. No way is that going to happen. I'm the boss, not the damn dog.

"Tonight was fun," I relent, against my better judgment.

"It was."

"Alright, well…" I hesitate. Then, because I'm a fucking idiot and the brain in my skull has been rattled loose, I lean down and brush my lips across her cheek, kissing her goodbye.

Oh my God. What the hell did I just do?

"What was that?" Spencer's eyes are as wide as saucers, fingers pressed to the spot on her skin where I pecked her.

"I don't know. I'm sorry."

"You're *sorry?*" She looks slightly injured by the apology.

Was that the wrong thing to say? I have no freaking clue anymore, but I do know kissing her on the fucking face was a horrible idea.

"I wasn't thinking, it just happened. Like kissing my mom goodbye."

Those wide eyes widen more.

"That's not what I meant."

"Phillip?"

"Yeah?"

Please don't punch me for talking out of my ass.

"Stop talking."

I stop talking.

The dog, bless his soul, nudges the back of my knee with his nose, a push toward the girl standing on her front porch, biting down on her bottom lip.

She's waiting for me to do something. Either turn around and walk back down those stairs, or…

…kiss her again. But this time like I mean it.

Don't do it, Bastard—you have a bet to win. Kissing her would be cheating, and then you'll have to lie to your friends—and to her—which only leads to more lying.

The truth costs nothing, but a lie could cost me everything.

And if I kiss her, that will cost me everything, too. No season tickets, no all-terrain vehicle, no timeshare.

But maybe I'd win something bigger—her.

Stop romanticizing losing, you loser.

What about all that bullshit about living in the moment people preach about? You only live once, etc., etc. I practice self-control on a daily basis, denying myself—junk food, and new relationships, apparently.

But wouldn't kissing her make things awkward tomorrow at to work?

It's going to be a tension-filled mess regardless—and at least we work in separate departments.

Spencer waits, hand now on the doorknob of her house. "Phillip?"

Nope. Not going to do it.

So caught up in the moment and our thoughts, neither of us noticed Humphrey and his slow stroll. Round and round and round the doggo must have walked, until the leash connected to his collar is wrapped around both our legs.

Spencer and I were standing close enough for the dog to confine our calves together. I move my left leg, attempting to shake it—but it's tangled.

I move a bit closer to Spencer because I have to in order to remedy the situation.

"What the…" She looks between our bodies at the twisted disorder. "If I didn't know any better, I'd say he did this on purpose."

That's a distinct possibility. I don't trust this dog—he's shady as fuck.

"You know, this awkwardness is worse than the time Bill Menzer asked to kiss me at the movies in eighth grade. There was no one else in the entire theater."

My mind momentarily leaves the tangle we find ourselves in, the dog panting happily at my feet. "What did you tell him?"

"I said no," she scoffs. "He was being a huge pussy about making his move, and that was a turn-off for me."

Oh Lord. Is she indirectly calling me a pussy because I kissed her on the cheek and not on the lips? Her faux-innocent, too-big smile confirms it.

Oddly enough, her smug attitude is turning me on.

"Don't be a pussy, Phillip," she goads. "Or do. Whichever."

"Was that a challenge?" I try to shuffle my feet.

Humphrey grumbles his displeasure: *Stay put, human.*

"Absolutely *not*. If a man is going to put his lips on mine, he better mean it."

She's so close I can smell her hair and perfume, and the takeout we had for dinner. "You're being really dramatic."

"No, *you* are."

Why is she so infuriating and argumentative? There is only one way to end this bickering so we can get on with our lives and I can stop obsessing over it, and that is for me to kiss her.

Obviously.

Plus, my little matchmaker approves.

Moving in, I slide my hand around her waist, over her jacket, the little gasp of surprise—and delight—spurring me on. So far, so good; she hasn't kneed me in the balls.

Yet.

"Well look at you taking charge," she teases, face tilting up, mouth inviting. "And just to be clear, this kiss means nothing."

"Don't steal my lines."

"I've kissed plenty of people—this is just us being curious."

No, this is us, tied together by a dog leash, wanting to make out on your front stoop, and I'm not sure why we're still talking.

Chances are, if you asked Spencer, she'd say this dallying was my fault.

"Spencer?"

"Huh?"

"Stop talking."

She stops talking. Slowly, I cover her mouth with mine, her

soft lips puckering. One kiss. Two. I draw back to regard her before kissing her again, our bottom lips pressed firmly together as our tongues introduce themselves.

Warm. Wet. Wanton.

Nice.

Comforting?

The kiss of a new friend.

It's cold outside, so steam rises with our every breath, drifting into the night sky. A car drives by and Humphrey grunts at it—not a protective sound but an excited one. He would chase the damn thing if he had the stamina for it.

He pulls on the leash, pushing at the back of my knee again with his snout, impatient and now frustrated by being part of the jumble. Makes strange snorting-sniffing-sneezing sounds in his throat. Dramatic and unnecessary.

Humphrey howls, once. Twice. Channeling his inner wolf.

Fuck.

Spencer breaks the kiss and looks down. "He's over it already."

Fucking dog is both a matchmaker and a cockblocker.

"He's an asshole." One who always thinks he's in charge. "There's a time and place for the howling, and he hasn't mastered the art of knowing when that is." So socially awkward.

"Aww, don't say that—look at those puppy dog eyes."

I look. "Yeah, yeah."

Bending at the waist, I attempt to walk Humphrey in the opposite direction, round and round our legs, Spencer's boobs knocking into my chest when the dog jostles us.

"Why is his leash so long?" she wonders out loud with a giggle and a shiver.

"I try to give the rat bastard freedom."

"It seems like he either wants to nap or cause chaos. There is no in between."

Now that he's been sprung free, the dog lumbers down the concrete steps, jerking at the blue lead impatiently.

I step back. "Guess I better get him home."

This fur monster has the worst timing—or maybe he just did me a colossal favor.

"Good night, Phillip." God*damn* I love the way she says my name. "Thanks again."

I make my way down the steps, shooting her a wave over my shoulder, stopping when Humphrey demands to sniff a tree trunk. And every single one of the wood chips surrounding it.

"Hey Phillip?" Spencer calls, and I turn to see her standing framed by her front door.

"Yeah?"

"It doesn't have to be weird at work tomorrow. So—don't make it weird."

Me? I'm not the awkward one here. "I wasn't planning on it. I was just going to tell *you* not to make it weird."

"Oh please." She tosses her ponytail, and even from here, I can see it shining. "It's only weird if it meant something."

What the fuck is that supposed to mean?

I don't have time to find out because the dog is tugging and tugging and tugging on his lead anxiously, now wanting to run toward home.

"Right. Only if it meant something."

"And we both know it didn't." She gives a definitive nod. "Because you don't date."

"Right."

I don't date.

14

HUMPHREY

I don't know who the girl was, but I liked her. Can you believe that? I liked her and she hasn't given me a single treat!

I made sure to give her a thorough sniff when she was on the ground at the house, lying down specially so I could kiss her face. I loved that about her.

I like how she scratched my ears and under my collar. I liked the sound of her voice and how she didn't scold me. I like how she talked in that high voice, even if I have no idea what she was saying.

Boy is carrying me again; I wasn't in the mood to hike and gave him the signal that I was done with the business of walking. He knows me so well, it's like we're the same person, even though if I were him, I would always carry snacks for me.

I sure do like when he carries me.

I sigh, drooling slightly as we trot along, having done my business and relieved myself. He had me cooped up all day, then there was no time for him to notice the spot where I peed next to the room where he stores my leash, but he'll see that later.

Oh well!

When Girl was chattering, I could feel Boy's hold on me getting tighter; she must have said something he didn't like, but my doggy heart was pounding so wildly from all the love I could have burst with joy.

Boy adores me so much.

We moved along at a snail's pace; Boy walks much slower when he's transporting me, his breathing as loud and labored as mine, especially when I see a squirrel.

We dropped Girl off at a dark house that looks a lot like the one I share with Boy; Girl pointed to it and stalled in front while I eyeballed the steps. They were concrete and cold, and I wasn't in the mood to climb them.

Then they ignored me, giving me no choice but to walk and walk and walk around them so they'd stop talking and press their faces together—until I began howling, forcing the attention back onto me.

I sigh.

Boy sets me on the ground with a grunt, rubbing my back. When he removes his hand, I protest.

"Humphrey, knock it off," he sternly warns, finally out of patience. "I'm losing patience with your bad behavior."

Fine. No more howling.

"You're a pain in the ass, do you know that? Do you?" Boy says as we turn and make our way home. "For once in your life, could you behave yourself?"

Words pour out of his mouth, but I ignore him. Besides, I only recognize half of the noises he makes—the other half I don't care one lick about.

"I swear, I'm going to send you to boot camp so you learn some manners."

No he won't.

"I mean it this time, Humphrey. You have to learn to listen."

No I don't.

"Blah blah blah ziptty blah blah do don't blah," he rants as we walk side by side, and I gaze up at him happily, content.

My rear wags as I meander along, sniffing my way home.

15

SPENCER

I brought in a cake today.

I told him I wasn't going to make it weird, so I did the one thing he wasn't going to misinterpret: food.

The way to a man's heart is through his stomach, though I'm in no way trying to get to his heart. Pfft. Me? No.

Fine. Yes.

I am—is that so wrong?

The kiss we shared last night was so-so, and I blame the dog; there wasn't any possibility of it deepening or getting passionate —not with Humphrey heaving and sighing at Phillip's feet.

Clam-jammer.

Phillip is late, which is no surprise. He could have a meeting, or he could be stuck in traffic, or perhaps the blasted dog was misbehaving.

I use the time to finish up my project, earbuds in, their noise-canceling feature on, soft music playing in my ears. I'm lost in my own world, shifting boxes on the grid on the screen. Tweaking colors. Sizing graphics up and down until it's perfect.

So perfect I think it might actually be done.

Sitting back in my seat to inspect it from a distance, I cross my arms and tilt my head, scrutinizing the design in an attempt to be unbiased, with a critical eye, as if I weren't the designer who just spent twelve hours piecing it together.

It's bold. Contemporary. Modern and clean.

Just like the company I work for. It isn't my personal style, but in my gut, I know I've hit a home run with this.

"Holy shit, that's good," says a deep voice from behind me, getting closer to my back. "Is it done?"

"I think so." I spin in my chair and get my first look at Phillip of the day: plaid shirt tucked into dark blue jeans, brown boots. Brown belt. It's a preppy, nerdier look than I'm used to from him, but masculine, sleeves rolled to the elbow.

I'm a sucker for well sculpted forearm.

He proceeds to set his things down on his desk, as he has every morning before, in the same methodical order: laptop slides out of its black sleeve. Computer glasses get set on top. Then, he pulls out and unwraps the computer cord, plugs it into the wall, other end into the side of the laptop. Opens the top. Adjusts the screen so it reflects less light.

Phillip pulls out the desk chair, shifting it to be positioned at an angle. Pulls out a water bottle, setting it to the left of the computer. Headphones. File folders and a pen.

Day after day, he goes through the same routine, one I've gotten used to and appreciate. It's comforting.

Cute.

I smile.

Then—he sees the cake.

I'm not saying I'm a genius or anything, but the look on Phillip's face when he sees the round, buttercream confection resting on the desk is priceless. Has me burying my face in the collar of my shirt to hide the smile.

"*Sorry for your loss*," he reads out loud through the square, clear window of the box. "Sorry for your loss. Very funny."

"I thought it was perfect for your last day before losing me."

I pause, pretending to study a cuticle on my index finger. "Let's be honest, you're going to be super bored next week."

He humors me with a smile. "That's probably true."

"Not probably." He will be.

I'm no expert on the subject, but I know when a guy is starting to develop feelings for me. The way Phillip studied me last night, unsure about whether or not he should make a move —every thought inside his body was displayed on his face. The furrowed brow. The downturned mouth. The tension in his broad shoulders as he looked down at me, at my lips.

Today he looks like a preppy lumbersexual, and I want to jump his bones.

God. That's something my mother would say about my dad.

I gag in my mouth a little at the thought of my parents banging.

"You must have been up all night—when did you have time to make this?"

Is he serious? "Aww, you're so cute—I bought the cake this morning then used a frosting pen to put the quote on it because I'm brilliant."

"You are kind of clever."

"Only kind of?" Even to my own ears, it sounds like I'm flirting. Should I dial the flirting down or turn it up? Decisions, decisions.

"Clever and intelligent—lethal combo."

"What about clever, intelligent, and beautiful?" I tease before I can change my mind.

"That too."

Question: if I call myself beautiful and a man agrees, is that as good as him actually calling me beautiful without being prompted? Or is he humoring me? Or am I overthinking this?

Answer: yes to all those things.

While Phillip continues getting situated, I text Miranda to be on the safe side.

Me: *Random question, are you busy?*

Miranda: *I'm always busy, but never too busy for you.*

Me: *That. Was. The. Sweetest.*

Miranda: *I know.*

Miranda: *What do you need, babe?*

Me: *If I call myself beautiful and a guy agrees with me, does that mean he thinks I'm beautiful or is he being polite?*

Miranda: *Probably both. But I'm not a dude, so how the hell am I supposed to know? Why, did Phillip call you beautiful?*

Me: *No, he called me clever and smart, then I made a joke, like, "And beautiful too ha ha" and he was like yeah.*

Miranda: *Why are you obsessing over this?*

Me: *He's leaving my office today and it's bumming me out. I thought maybe he'd ask me out.*

Miranda: *Spencer, it is nine in the morning.*

Me: *It gets worse.*

Miranda: *How?*

Me: *I brought him a cake.*

Miranda: *A CAKE? WHY?*

Me: *Okay first of all, stop yelling. Second of all, it's a going away cake and it's hilarious. He likes it.*

Miranda: *I will never understand you.*

Me: *HE LIKES FOOD.*

Miranda: *OMFG. Stop.*

Me: *Sorry. I feel so middle school about this whole thing.*

Miranda: *Well you haven't liked a boy since eighth grade, so this all makes sense. You're relationship-ly stunted.*

Me: *I am not, you sasshole. Stop making up words.*

Miranda: *But that's how words are created—we make them up.*

Me: *Can we not stray from the point?*

Miranda: *Knowing what your point is would be incredibly helpful in that endeavor…*

Me: *Why are you like this?*
Miranda: *I was born this way. **flips hair***
Me: *Bye.*
Miranda: *You'll come back—you always do.*
Me: *BYE.*

16

PHILLIP

"Who has you scowling?"

Spencer has had a frown on her face for the past few minutes.

"Who were you texting?" I blurt out, unable to stop seeking information about her, curious. "Who pissed you off?"

Please don't say your boyfriend.

Not that I would care. If I thought for one second she had a boyfriend, I wouldn't have kissed her. I wouldn't be obsessing— this daydreaming about her is not going to win me a bet.

Don't be a fucking dumbass, Phillip. If she had a boyfriend, she would not have let you kiss her last night. She would have told you to fuck off.

Or. Not?

My head gives a shake; she isn't the cheating type—I definitely would have known if she was spoken for. I would never have kissed her or touched her if I suspected for one second she was in a relationship.

Besides, she's been fishing for details on my love life for days.

"Miranda. You remember her, from The Basement? She's the worst."

My body relaxes, tension I didn't know I was holding

causing my shoulders to sag as it dissipates. I sink back down into my chair.

"Ahh." I give a nod of sympathy because I understand what it's like having friends who are a royal pain in the ass.

There must be something in the water because Blaine and Brooks have been blowing up my phone this morning, too. Nagging. Continuous questions about Spencer and our association—neither of them believe there is nothing going on between us, but Blaine has an ulterior motive: winning the Bastard Bachelor bet.

I glance at my laptop to see the iMessage group chat popping up on the screen, ignoring most of them. The pair of them are doing just fine holding a conversation without me.

Blaine: *What's going on with that chick from work?*
Brooks: *He said nothing but he's full of shit.*
Blaine: *Agree. We saw the way she was looking at you, dude. She looked thirsty.*

Thirsty? What the fuck?

Messages continue popping up, but I ignore them, shifting my focus to Spencer. "Are we sharing this cake with anyone or pigging out on it ourselves?"

"Up to you—it's your cake."

"So I can just take it home without sharing?"

Spencer narrows her eyes. "Technically, you could."

"But?"

"Then I'd have to kill you." An imaginary angel halo floats above her pretty head. "I brought a serving knife."

"You would."

"Sue me for liking cake."

Her hair is down today and curlier than I've seen it. She's wearing blue—my favorite color. She looks pretty, and I wasn't fucking around when I told her she's beautiful.

Or alluded to it when she jested about it.

Weak not to come out and say it to her face, but I can't risk her getting overly attached.

Then why did you kiss her, fucker?

Because I'm selfish.

And I like her.

Ugh. A lot.

How did I not know she was here, under my nose, the entire time I've been working here? If I had known, there's a good chance we would already be in a relationship and I would never have agreed to that dumb bet in the first place.

Brooks forfeited—you can, too.

Brooks makes more money than I do. He can afford to give up the valuable tickets and timeshare and four-wheeler; I can't. My plan is to sell that shit and make a profit, maybe buy another piece of real estate and use it as income property.

Brooks will kill me when I sell the baseball season tickets—seasonal seats for the Jags are impossible to come by; families wait years for a chance to buy them, which doesn't come often because they can be passed down from generation to generation.

Still, if I can make six figures selling them...

It's less of a risk than the start of a new relationship. What if it fizzles and fades, and we break up and I'm left with nothing? No girlfriend, no income property. I will have given it up for nothing.

There are no guarantees.

My laptop pings again with more messages, coming in one after the other consecutively. It's obnoxious and annoying.

Brooks: *For real though, bro, if you LIKE her forget about the fucking bet.*
Blaine: *Agree. Definitely forget about the fucking bet. I'm going to win it anyway—you have failure written all over you. Date her.*
Brooks: *You can sleep with her and still win. There is no rule about fucking a girl, you just can't date her exclusively.*

Blaine: *Shut up, asshole, don't encourage him.*
Brooks: *This from the guy who broke up with his girlfriend to win a bet.*
Blaine: *My level of commitment is legendary. Neither of you can say the same.*
Brooks: *We don't know if Philly Cheesesteak is going to dump this chick or not—it ain't over until the chick is crying from having her heart shit on.*
Blaine: *He won't dump her—he doesn't want this bad enough.*
Brooks: *Why are we even talking about this? We were trying to decide if we were going out this weekend—Abbott has plans with her grandparents so I'm a free man.*
Blaine: *You want to have a club meeting THIS WEEKEND? Lame.*

The messages go on and on and on, the two of them arguing.

"Wow. You thought my face was serious?" Spencer's voice interrupts my thoughts. "What is going through that mind of yours? Yikes."

"Nothing," I lie. "This project is just stressing me out."

Liar, liar, liar.

"Why don't we eat cake? Would that make you feel better?"

No. That would go against yet another rule of mine: eating anything non-breakfast-like before noon. "Yeah, sure."

She smiles prettily. "I know you have a rule about eating a real meal before dessert, but cake always makes everything better, especially before lunch. You run and get some plates and napkins and I'll cut it, okay?"

Sounds good to me.

I stand, pushing my chair back, then push it back in so it's out of her way when she comes around to cut the cake. I'm halfway to the breakroom before I realize I've been humming all the way down the aisle.

There are a few people around when I get there, making coffee or eating baked goods, casually shooting the shit.

Two of them are from the purchasing department, which I'll resume more contact with once my shit is moved back into my office space.

"...that hellhole. All she does is blow her nose and cough. One more day and I would have been wearing a mask."

"That's not as bad as sharing a room with Pete. If he makes one phone call, he makes eighty, Jesus Christ."

I sidle up to Dan and Roger, interrupting their bitch-fest. "Hey guys. Just grabbing plates—my officemate brought in a cake."

Dan looks confused. "Cake? For what?"

Duh. "For me." I'm not proud to say I'm bragging. Sounds like they had bad luck in the officemate department this week while I hit the jackpot. "It's a going away cake, and I'm in charge of plates."

"I want cake," Roger says. "Who are you sharing with and why didn't you say anything sooner?"

"Her name is Spencer. She's one of the leads in marketing."

"And she brought you cake?" Dan remains dubious. "Why?"

"It's a going away cake," I repeat. "Because we move back to our own offices after today."

"What's her deal? Is she old?"

"No, she's my age." After I've collected the items I need, I also grab two bottles of water.

"I'm confused. Cake makes no sense."

I clap him on the shoulder. "That's why you're a numbers guy, Dan. We don't pay you to be pretty."

Dan is an estimator; he draws up the bids we use when we're trying to win jobs. He measures, records, and calculates without an ounce of creativity in his entire dad bod.

Whatever.

I have cake to eat.

I give them and everyone else a head bob, retreating to

Spencer's office, whistling, with pep in my step. Give a glance down the hallway where my office is and spot numerous carpenters still hard at work, on the floor, on their knees, pressing the new carpet flat.

Mmm, smells like melted plastic and fiber.

Two plates, two napkins, two forks, and two water bottles are balanced in my arms when I round the corner to the north side. I can see Spencer's ass in the wide window, and I can't tell if she's hunched over my desk or still cutting the cake, but her backside looks spectacular in the jeans she has on.

I'm not typically one to objectify anyone, but I'm certainly appreciating this view.

Now she has her hands on her hips.

Okay—definitely not cutting the cake.

I give the metal doorframe a rap with my knuckles. "Knock-knock, I come bearing sundries."

She doesn't turn to face me or move from her spot. I'm not sure what to do with myself, so I stand stationary, rooted to the threshold.

"Am I a part of some bet?" is the first thing she says, quietly.

"What are you talking about?" I know damn well what she's talking about and curse myself for leaving my laptop open.

"Your messages. They popped up while you were gone. I wasn't snooping, but it kept pinging," she says defensively. "Be honest—am I part of some bet?"

Fuck.

Fuck, fuck, fuck!

"Why would you think you were part of some bet?"

"I'm not blind—obviously your friends are talking about me. Unless there's another office roomie you've been shacking up with." She finally steps away and moves to the left, shimmying back to her side of the mega-desk. "You hardly even flirt with me, let alone date me. I don't understand why they would think you were going to dump me. It makes no sense."

She's terrible at putting two and two and two together, but

I'm not going to fill in the blanks for her. Unfortunately for me, Spencer isn't going to let this go, and I send up a silent prayer that this discussion doesn't escalate into a full-blown argument.

"So there is a club," she says softly. It's a statement, not a question.

I gape like a deer in headlights, unsure how to react. I go with an intelligent, "Uh."

"I'll take that as a yes." Spencer begins shuffling papers and reorganizing the pens, markers, and paper clips on her desk. Starts scribbling on the desktop calendar, which I'm assuming is utter nonsense. She's avoiding me.

"I mean…I don't know what to say."

"No need. Your boys did plenty of talking for you." She slashes the calendar with a bright neon pink marker. "Let's see, what was it they were saying…" She taps her chin with the marker, the cap still off.

I don't tell her she has a pink chin; I don't want her to bite my head off.

"Oh, now I remember!" She clears her throat. Deepens her voice. "*You can sleep with her and still win. There is no rule about fucking a girl, you just can't date her exclusively.*"

Wow. Talk about a photographic memory.

I'm impressed she rattled that off verbatim.

"Classy. You guys are reeeal classy."

Crap.

Fuck.

I open my mouth but flounder like a guppy.

"Close your mouth, Phillip—you're letting the flies out."

Whoa. "That was harsh."

"Well." She tilts her neon pink chin. "You deserve it, don't you think?"

My hands go up defensively. "In all fairness, I didn't lie to you. I made no promises, made no moves on you, did nothing but work alongside you for the past week. I wasn't inappropriate—"

"You kissed me. What was that all about? If that wasn't you making a move, what are we calling it?"

"I—"

"Or do you go around kissing people you don't care about? You play games?"

"I—"

"Stop talking, Phillip. Nothing you say is going to please me right now. Nothing. Just leave me alone and let me cool off." Her blue eyes stray to my laptop and workstation. "Consider gathering your things."

My lips press together and I bow my head. Sit. Make eye contact with the cake, which she's removed from the box and sliced into. I can see the fresh frosting—I can smell it. Buttery creamy goodness. My mouth actually waters.

"Does this mean I don't get cake?"

Spencer glares. "No you do not get cake, you ass!"

"But…" It's my cake. She said so. "Why?"

"Because it's my cake."

"It was a gift." To me.

"But I bought it."

"That's not how gifts work—ask any lawyer."

"I'm going to *strangle* you," she threatens, her with the pink chin and angry eyes.

Damn. Miss Angry Pants looks gorgeous when she's murderous.

"Don't make empty threats," I taunt, knowing it's going to fuel her fire.

"Don't talk to me."

"Your chin is pink." I smirk as I deliver the news.

Her head whips in my direction, eyes blue pools of anger. "What?" It's obvious she doesn't believe me; she's too busy hating my guts.

"You wrote all over your chin when you were tapping it with the marker." I grin, pleased to be ruining her moment.

"Why the hell didn't you say anything?"

"I'm telling you now! And you told me to stop talking."

Spencer loudly scoffs as if I am her cross to bear. "Please, when do you ever listen to anything I have to say?"

"Chin's still pink," I prod.

"Shut. Up. Phillip."

"It is."

"I'll handle it! Quit bringing it up."

"Just don't want you to forget."

Abruptly, she stands, hands planted on her desk. "Thank goodness we didn't take our harmless flirtation any further. I cannot stand the sight of you right now. You and your friends are despicable." She rounds the desk and storms out of the office, rubbing her face with the fabric of her shirtsleeve.

My heart is damn near beating out of my chest.

I breathe in. I breathe out.

Just relax. Let her cool off.

My attention turns to my laptop screen. I give my mouse pad a tap to bring it to life and glare at the chat box in the center.

Fucking Blaine and Brooks, this is—

It's not their fault and you know it.

It's yours for having your head up your ass. For being indecisive and stubborn. For lying to your friends.

Blaine: *Our boy has gotten quiet—what do you think he's doing?*

Brooks: *I know what he's NOT doing—that girl at his office he's afraid of.*

Blaine: *I smell a loser...*

Oh my fucking God, did Spencer see this?

No wonder she's pissed.

My face is on fire, flaming hot as I read line after line of inappropriate messages.

With an angry click, I slam my laptop closed.

17

SPENCER

I stride back into the office, stalk to his side of the room, and lift the cake. Unceremoniously dump it in the trash.

He gasps. "Hey! Why did you do that?!"

"If you think I'm letting you eat MY CAKE, you are delusional!"

"That's wasteful!"

"Really? Is it? Because I really do not give a shit!" I stare into the trash, where blue and red frosting are smeared on the garbage bag, lining the side on its way to perdition. I retrieve the bin from the floor and thrust it toward him. "You want some cake? Help yourself."

Seeing those messages on his laptop, while I was slicing a cake I brought in special, for him? Gut-wrenching. Embarrassing. Horrifying.

I've never felt humiliated, not even the time I had my period in middle school while wearing white jeans. I had blood on my butt and walked around the halls that way until my math teacher told me to use the bathroom, clean myself up.

I borrowed a giant maxi pad liner from my friend Vanessa, but the damage had already been done.

"Spencer…"

"Don't." I'm so angry. "Just. Don't."

I know all the things he's going to say. I know, because despite the texts and weird way he's acted when I questioned him about the jacket, and the club—I trust that he's not a complete prick.

And he's right—he never made any inappropriate advances at work, never overstepped, never said anything off-putting. I never felt uncomfortable.

I only felt...

The stirrings of.

Of.

No, not *that*.

Not so soon.

No.

I'm not that naïve.

And he is not that callous.

None of this was intentional.

Was it bad timing? Yes. Was it in bad taste?

So much yes.

He has his things collected, packing up after lunch. The manager of his department came around to notify him that his office was ready, said if he wanted to call it an early day, he could. His desk and furniture would all be back in place by Monday morning.

Great.

Fantastic.

He can leave, so that's what he does.

Hovering in the door, it's clear he hasn't a clue what his last words are going to be. So he says nothing at all—just looks at me long and hard, the expression on his face wiped clean. I can't read his mind and I can't read his face, but I can avert my gaze and read my computer screen.

I stare at it until the last rustle of his pants and shirt and breathing fade away.

18

PHILLIP

"I hate you both."

Pretty sure I'm slurring my words, but they're still making sense, so I hardly care. We're at The Basement after I called an emergency meeting, sans velvet smoking jackets.

Desperate times call for desperate measures.

"You've told us that thirteen times already," Blaine says. "I'm keeping track."

"Wow. Could you be any more unsupportive?"

My friends glance at each other.

"I saw that." Fuckers.

"You still haven't told us what this is about, but I'm willing to bet it has something to do with that girl." Brooks glances toward Blaine, neither of them sober themselves. "Wush her name? Spender?"

"Spencer," I correct him.

"That's a guy's name," Brooks argues.

"It's a girl's name. How about you shut up, your girlfriend has a last name for a first name."

Their eyes get wide; of the three of us, I'm the least confrontational. Always the least likely to tell anyone how I feel. This outburst gives them pause, drunk as we are.

"Did you dump her?" Blaine is finally eating some food, the appetizers we ordered when we sat down.

"We weren't together."

"Do you wanna be together?" Blaine holds his fingers into the A-OK gesture and uses the index finger of his other hand to poke through the hole he's making.

Idiot.

"Yes." I hesitate, unable to prevent the truth from flowing out of my mouth. "I like her."

"Enough to forfeit?"

Maybe.

No.

"Maybe?" My elbows rest on my knees and I lean forward, burying my face in my hands. "Ugh, I feel sick."

"If you're going to spew, do it in the bathroom, dude," Brooks offers unhelpfully.

I glance over at him. "I'm not going to puke, I just feel sick."

Why is this room so fucking loud? I can't hear myself think.

"What am I going to do?" I groan.

"I don't know, bro—what do you want to do?" Blaine asks, and the weight of a hand is on my back, pressing down to comfort me. "Just tell us what you need."

Oh, now he's being sensitive? Where was this caring, helpful fuck a half-hour ago when I started downing shots?

"Right this second, I give zero shits about the bet, or the season tickets or the anything." My head starts to pound, so I raise it. "I fucked up."

They patiently wait for the floodgate to open.

Sighing, I take the glass of water that's magically appeared out of nowhere and chug down a healthy swallow. It's cold and refreshing and just what I needed.

"The truth is, I don't know what I want."

The gravity of my statement hangs above us.

Again, they wait.

"I...think if I don't fix this thing with Spencer, it'll be too late, and I...worry that..."

What do I worry, what do I worry?

Focus, Phillip. *Focus.*

Two fingers press into my temples as I search for the right words. "I worry that...she thinks she's the butt of some joke. No, that's not it." Inhale. Exhale. "I worry if I don't choose her, I'm going to regret it."

"How long have you known her?" Brooks asks. "Four days? You're going to blow a bet for someone you've known four days? You cannot be that stupid."

Blaine smacks him in the arm. "Dude, I'm not just saying this because I'm drunk—I'm saying it because I love you." His hand moves to rest on my arm. "And I'm not saying it because I want to win the bet, which I do."

"Would you get to the point?" Brooks grumbles, annoyed.

"That's all I had to say."

I look at Brooks. "I don't think whether I've known her four days or four weeks or four months matters. I just have this feeling about her—you know?"

Brooks sighs. "Yeah. Unfortunately, I do know."

"She's a good person, I know it."

"Do you? Know it? Do you know and he knows and everyone knows?" Blaine cackles. "Oh my God, you two are so toasted."

"God you're a pain in the ass."

I have no idea what I'm trying to say. My friends aren't wrong; I did just meet Spencer. I just...

From the second that first crumb fell from her mouth to her sweater, I knew.

I mean—I wanted to put a muzzle on her, and she drove me nuts, and was hella distracting, and come to think of it, what did I actually get done this week? Nothing. Nothing got submitted or reported and I visited exactly zero job sites. Visited zero subcontractor showrooms, looked at zero materials.

I groan.

She's already making me weak; the only thing I've had any desire to do this week is spend time with her. The fact that I was jammed into her cramped space? That made it effortless.

I miss her.

I hate knowing I hurt her. I hate *knowing* she thinks I'm a flaming bag of dog shit.

"What should I do?" 'Cause right now I want to shrivel up and die. "Forfeit?"

The more thought I give that idea, the more it appeals to me. Being a member of this club hasn't benefitted me once; it's done nothing but make me miserable.

I can liberate myself. Instead, I'm full of libations.

Ugh.

"You're not forfeiting," Brooks tells me authoritatively.

"But it worked for you."

"Yeah, but I was in love. You're in like—it's too soon."

Is it though? "I need to talk to her about this."

"Definitely drunk-text her," Blaine suggests vehemently, biting into a mozzarella stick. "That always gets the conversation rolling in the right direction."

"Do *not* listen to him," Brooks counters. "Do not."

"I haven't drunk-texted anyone since I had a flip phone," I inform them, staring down at the phone number I got from the company directory. "Plus, it's not my style."

"What is your style?" they both want to know.

"I don't know."

But I'm going to figure it out.

19

SPENCER

The kitchen sparkles and shines.

The bathroom? Twinkles.

I can now see my reflection in every surface of my apartment, including the fabric ones. I've scrubbed every nook and cranny from top to bottom.

Twice.

I don't throw pity parties. I don't wallow. And I don't whine. So what do I do when I'm angry and upset?

Clean.

Quick, someone check my temperature—I'm coming down with something!

I rest my hip on the corner of the couch and let out a sigh, the first deep breath I've taken since yesterday at the office. It seems as if I've been holding it since the moment Phillip walked out without looking back.

Jerk.

You're the fool…

I knew it was a huge mistake to entertain the idea of a work romance, and my gut was correct. Did I listen? No. Thank goodness it was only the span of a week, and not weeks or months. I can't imagine how much harm that would have done.

There's a rag in my hand and sweat on my brow. I blow the stray strands of hair out of my face and glance around the living room. It's never been neater. Totally decluttered. A pile of crap I no longer want or need sits by the front door, waiting to be placed in totes—which I'll have to run out and get this weekend. The donation center will be happy to see me; the taxi cab driver who has to haul all this shit there with me? Not so much.

Tearing through my apartment should have felt cathartic, and it did, for an entire three hours. Now that the adrenaline has worn off, though, all I'm left with are my thoughts.

Overthink it, overthink it, my brain screams.

No worries! Got that part covered...

Ruefully, I smile. Heavily, I sigh again, unsure about what to do next. Pack everything into plastic bags until I can run to the store for totes? Leave the piles where they are? Start rearranging the bookshelves in my tiny home office?

Maybe I should arrange my books by color rather than author and series. Would that just frustrate me if I have to search for a specific title? *Book nerd problems.*

I move from my perch in the living room, into the kitchen, and scowl at the pigeons shitting on my windowsill. Are they pretty birds? Absolutely. Are they ruining the aesthetic of my view? Also yes.

"Shoo!" I instruct the little family of gray poultry.

They ignore me.

"I said git!"

Why do I care? They're here every damn day, pooping on the wooden ledge, messing it up with twigs and grass and poo.

My shoulders sag, defeated, and a sniffle escapes my throat. First one tear, then another, until I'm searching for a tissue to wipe my nose with.

"Ugh, what is wrong with you?!" My question is to absolutely no one. "I'm going to be alone forever!" Dramatically, I plop down into a chair at my little round table. I normally love my cute apartment, but today? I feel alone and isolated.

Unloved.

Even Miranda couldn't cheer me up with a midmorning invitation for breakfast.

Not today, I told her.

Miranda: *How about a movie later?*
Me: *I don't know—I'll think about it.*
Me: *Why am I acting like this? Like it's the end of the world? Why does my stomach hurt and my heart ache?*
Miranda: *Because…maybe Phillip is your soul mate. Have you thought of that?*

That.

That gave me pause.

What if Miranda is right? Is that why I've been on a roller coaster of emotion since the moment Phillip and I bumped into each other Monday morning, since I watched as he puked in the trash? I remember feeling bad for him—wanting to comfort him even though I knew he'd be too embarrassed to accept the help.

I tap on my phone and scroll for the music app. Swipe and click, pairing the device to my wireless speaker and searching for an upbeat ditty. What I need is a song to lift my spirits.

A ballad will make me cry.

So will country.

This one about a slow dance in a parking lot? Cue the tears!

This one? Too romantic.

This one? Depressing.

I wind up listening to a podcast, *Love & Sex with Doctor Stacy,* but who am I trying to kid? I'm neither having sex nor am I in love.

"*Communication, from the beginning of a relationship, is key. With it, you're setting yourself and your relationship up for success—successful communication,*" the host of the podcast drones on. "*Leads to a healthy sex life if you can tell your partner what you desire and need.*"

Well. Big fail on the open and honest part.

"Let's open up the phone lines for a few callers."

I listen for the next hour while I remove all the books from the white bookcase, piling myriads of paperbacks on the floor around the room in neat stacks, dusting the shelves.

Finally content, I hum.

Further along, I turn off the podcast and switch to music.

I'm in a zone, an organizing fool, when the door buzzer sounds from below. Three levels down, someone is pushing on the monitor.

Bzz.

Bzz, bzz.

"Who on earth?" I set down the stack of paperbacks cradled in my arms and rise, wiping my hands off on the thighs of my jeans.

I'm not expecting anyone, and my intercom almost never buzzes—mainly because the only one who comes over is Miranda, and she has the door code.

Bzz.

"Alright, alright, I'm coming!"

This better be good—or the wrong address. Perhaps a package I forgot I ordered? Nah, the mail guy usually leaves those on the first floor.

My pink nail hits the gray button located next to my front door.

"Hello?"

"Hey," says a deep, male voice.

"Uh." I don't recognize it. "Who is this?"

The intercom static crackles. "Phillip."

"Oh."

It's Phillip.

"What do you want?"

"I have... I want..."

I listen to stagnant air as he pauses awkwardly.

"I have a peace offering. I was hoping…" He pauses again. "I was hoping you didn't hate me enough to not let me come up."

My ears perk up. Optimism fills my chest. "A peace offering, you say?"

"Yes, and it's getting heavy."

Heavy? What the hell could it be?

I press the button again. "Is Humphrey with you?"

He laughs through the speaker. "God no. He's a mood-killer."

That he is. But he's also adorable and silly. "What peace offering?"

"You have to let me up to find out."

Hmm. "That sounds like blackmail."

"No, it's bribery."

"You and your bribes—ugh, I can't."

"So…will you buzz me in?"

I bite my bottom lip indecisively. "I guess I can let you up. No funny business."

I press the door release, granting him entry, heart palpitating. Oh my God, what in the world is he doing here? What does he want? What does my hair look like and *why the hell didn't I put on makeup this morning?!*

Rushing to the bathroom mirror, I fluff my mop of a hairdo then fumble for a hair tie. Pull it back and hate the way it looks. Let it loose and finger-comb it.

"Ugh!" *Dammit!*

No makeup. Sweat. I dash to the bathroom and fumble for a wash rag, wet it, and stick it under my T-shirt, washing my pits. Give myself a good douse of body spray, certain it now reeks to floral heaven in my apartment.

Why am I like this?!

No time to answer the question as I have to answer the soft knocking at my front door. Giving myself one more look in the mirror, I give up entirely. Rosy cheeks will have to do.

I count to three before pulling the handle. Paste on a neutral expression—it's never a good idea to appear too eager.

But then...I smile, because: Phillip.

"Hey." His own smile is sheepish and shy.

He's carrying a small bakery box. Pink. Mysterious, as there is no clear viewing window in the top.

"Hi." I rest my hip on the doorjamb. "Whatcha got there?"

I don't mince words; I'm curious—about why he's here and what's in the box.

I love pink. I hope it's cupcakes.

If that's the case, all will be forgiven. I'm cheap and easy and have no shame in my game. I'll admit it: will break for cake.

"Can I come in?"

I move aside. "You're not content standing on my stoop?"

Seeing him in my kitchen is surreal; I haven't had a man inside my apartment in months, possibly a year, and the sight of it is strange—especially since we only just met. We only just kissed.

We fought at work yesterday.

I was glad to be gone at the end of the day, knowing when I return on Monday, his things will be gone, but then again—so will mine. I have no clue whose space I will be sharing, or if I'll elect to work from home.

My boss gave us the choice.

Phillip isn't the biggest dude I've ever seen, but his presence fills my room all the same. Broad shoulders and the perfect amount of bulk, he's dressed casually in jeans, a T-shirt, and a navy fleece jacket.

He sets the pink box on my table and shrugs off his jacket.

Dang—he must intend to stay a while.

Nosey, I give that box the stare-down.

Briefly, he rubs his hands together, nervous. "First, I want to start by saying I'm sorry."

"For?"

His lips quirk. "A lot of things. I've been doing a lot of soul searching in the past twenty-four hours, self-reflecting."

I plop down on the sofa and cross my arms. "That sounds serious."

He continues standing. "The whole thing with my friends started as a joke. Kind of. Brooks was upset about a breakup, was angry and hurt and needed an outlet for his frustration."

"He couldn't have joined a basketball league?" I quip, to Phillip's ire.

He ignores me. "One night we were all at The Basement getting drunk, and we were on a roll. The whole club thing came up, and we started spouting off rules. Then someone—I can't remember who—decided we should have stakes, so the three of us had to pony up a possession. Mine is an all-terrain vehicle. If I lose the bet, I lose the four-wheeler."

He clears his throat to continue as I listen.

"Blaine broke up with his girlfriend, my sister ordered us those matching smoking jackets—we were all in."

"Blaine broke up with his *girlfriend*?" My eyes are out of their sockets I'm gaping so hard. "That's horrible."

"She was horrible, but that's a story for another day."

"But who does that?"

"Guys. Immature ones."

"Are you admitting you're immature?"

He nods. "One hundred percent."

"At least we agree."

"Can I finish apologizing?"

I give him a head bob worthy of the Queen of England. "Go on."

Phillip rolls his eyes but smiles. "Our club—which I'm not supposed to be telling you about—was fine at first. We'd meet, shoot the shit, have drinks. At first it didn't seem like anyone was going to lose, because none of us were dating. Blaine didn't even seem interested in reconciling with Bambi."

"Hold up—her name was Bambi?" *Shit, he should have known that wasn't going to last.*

"Then one night, Brooks cracks. He'd met someone, his neighbor, Abbott. She blew him off a few times and—"

"Blew him off! Did he know her?"

He stares blankly. "Not blow jobs—she gave him the cold shoulder."

"Oh." Oops. "That does seem more plausible in this scenario."

"Ya think? So we're at The Basement and he's distraught—like I was last night…"

My brows go up, interested. What's this now, he was distraught? About what?

"…and he confessed he'd fallen in love, He forfeited the bet, lost his family's season tickets to the Jags."

"How romantic!" My chest constricts with the idea of a man giving up material possessions for love. I clutch my hand to my heart and add an, "Aww."

"Brooks was the first to fall, so then it was Blaine and me."

"Wait, can I quickly ask—did y'all actually make him give you his baseball tickets?"

"Fuck yeah, they're incredible seats."

Men.

No girl would do that to her friend. They would romanticize the situation and disband the club, but nope—not these bastards.

"So then what happened?" I'm on the edge of my seat. How does this relate to me?

"I'm getting there. Hold your horses."

"Sorry." I slide my pinched fingers across my lips.

"I'm apologizing because you saw messages that obviously weren't intended for you—the club was never intended to hurt anyone."

"Except Bambi," I mumble sarcastically.

He silences me with a bemused glance, beginning to pace

briskly in my small living room. "I'm sorry about those fucking messages. I know most of them were from my buddies, but it still made me feel like shit that you had to see them."

They certainly made me feel like shit.

"And I know we technically just met, but that doesn't mean I haven't been thinking about you nonstop. I haven't slept since Tuesday. I wonder what movies you like and if you like vacations. Do you love road trips or flying? Margarita or Bloody Mary? What scares you? Movies at home or in the theater?"

He volleys question after question as if on autopilot, as if he's been making mental lists and memorizing them.

In five long strides, he's in the kitchen and back, clutching the pink box.

Stands in front of me, drops one knee down to the carpet. "Spencer, in the five days I've known you, I've never been more frustrated or embarrassed in my entire life. I've also never laughed so hard, and you're the reason why. I want to start over —minus the part where you witness me throwing up in a garbage can—and get to know you."

Phillip hesitates dramatically, popping the top of the pink bakery box.

"Spencer Standish from the marketing department, would you make me the happiest purchasing manager in the company and consider dating me?"

I glance down.

Pink box. Pink cake. Pink frosting with the words:

I LIKE YOU. AND NAPS.

Stop it. Stop it right now, this is the sweetest thing I've ever seen.

My insides melt.

"When did you have time to make this?" I tease, biting my bottom lip. If I don't, I'll grin myself stupid, cheeks already aching.

"I ran and got it this morning, had the girl behind the counter add the words. I know you like cake."

I do. Cake and *kisses*.

I lean forward and plant one on the tip of his nose. Mmm.

"It's to replace the one you threw in the trash," he explains. "The one we didn't get to eat because you're stubborn as fuck."

"Oh my God." My hand flies to my mouth to stifle a giggle, but deep down inside, I don't care. He one hundred percent deserved to have that glorious cake tossed in the garbage. "Please, let's just acknowledge that whole situation wasn't your finest moment and move on."

"Agree. But I still can't believe you wasted a perfectly good cake."

"Can I confess something to you?"

"Of course."

"After you left the office, I dug the cake out of the trash and ate half of it." I laugh, remembering how jacked up the cake was, frosting staining my shirtsleeve after I fished it out of the bin. "So delicious."

"You ate cake from the garbage," he deadpans.

"Uh, hi—it was a twenty-five-dollar cake." My chin tilts defiantly. "I'd do it again. With or without a fork."

"You are really something."

"I take that as a compliment, thank you."

"You're so fucking cute." He meets me halfway for another kiss—a real one this time, on the mouth.

I reach between us and dip the tip of my finger in the cake. Swipe up a dollop of frosting and lick it.

Our mouths meet again, sugary sweet, and Phillip moans. "God you taste good."

"I like cake and naps." I groan when he deepens the kiss. "And nerds from the purchasing department who are good at math."

"I am really good at math, and measuring and stuff."

Sexy talk.

Suddenly, a thought occurs to me, and I pull back to look at him. "Phillip—you want to date me, but it's against club rules.

Does that mean…" My voice trails off and I want to squash the hope in my tone.

"I forfeited? Yeah."

"You did not." I couldn't stop my heart from racing at this information if my nerves put up a roadblock.

"I did."

"Why?! You literally just met me—are you crazy?" But if it's true, this is absolutely the most romantic thing anyone has ever done for me.

We've only known each other five days.

When you know, you know, my gran used to say. I never knew what she meant until this exact moment, staring down at Phillip as he kneels on my living room rug. With a cake.

"I might be. Every ounce of common sense I possess tells me this is illogical, and forfeiting is a huge gamble—next week we may decide we can't stand each other and I'm out everything. But what if one week turns into a month and a month turns into a year?"

My heart.

It's. Going. To. Burst.

"Yeah?" I can scarcely get the word out, so breathless.

"Yeah." He wiggles the cake cover. "What do you think, Spencer? Do you want to give it a go?"

Do I give in this easily, or should I make him work harder for it? I'm a sucker for men who humble themselves—and pretending I don't want to date him would be a lie.

God he turns me on.

Yes I want to give it a go. "Okay, Phillip. Let's date."

"Let's date the shit out of each other. Nothing half-assed."

Well then.

Never one to shy away from physical touch, I pucker my lips as an invitation—best he learns now to lavish me with affection.

Best learn now that I'm a bit bossy.

"Do we want to cut the cake? I can grab forks…"

He gives me a look. "You *just* got done telling me you ate cake out of the trash—want to just use our fingers?"

"That could get...dirty." I wiggle my eyebrows in a creepy way, hoping he'll read it as sexual. Not that I want him to get the wrong idea about me and my morals, but—

I'm a sure thing.

We kiss again, tongues sweet from the frosting on my finger, and it occurs to me that I could kiss him forever, he tastes that good. Smells amazing. His hands? Magic.

Big, strong, and capable, Phillip's hands stroke my shoulders, then my arms, lazily moving up and down, then up again. Stroke my neck. Brush through my hair.

They slide to my face, cupping my cheeks gently as his mouth expertly moves over mine.

I squirm, desperate to feel more than just his hands in my hair, on my face, on my arms. I want to feel his hands on my boobs, between my legs.

Giving him a gentle push, I move to join him on the floor, cake still in its box, resting beside us. I swipe more frosting onto my thumb, brush it across his bottom lip.

Lean in and suck it off. "You know what else I can do with this frosting?" I whisper into his ear, licking the outer shell.

"What?" he croaks.

"Mmm," is my only answer, hungry for dessert before the main course. Greedy fingers move to the front of Phillip's jeans.

"God yes," he groans as I fumble for the button and tug, dragging down his zipper. "Too fast? I don't want to rush you."

"Too slow."

I want to do this, have wanted to since he strolled inside my apartment, unsure, and pleaded his case. Said all those soulful, beautiful words. Got down on bended knee to ask for permission to date me.

While I work his pants, Phillip works my shirt, tugging the hem up, and I thank God I'm wearing pretty underwear and a cute bra. Because a few of my panties? Hideous.

Somehow we end up lying on my carpet, methodically stripping down to nothing. Skin and heat, this new boyfriend of mine. His body is glorious. Hot flesh, just the right amount of hair and muscle. Not too hard but not too soft.

Imperfectly perfect, just like me.

My right hand glides down his chest, over his beautiful abs. Pelvis. I eye his erection with a watering mouth, frost my index finger and run it down the length of his cock.

He inhales, holding his breath, one hand rubbing my back.

I maneuver my body over his, lower my head, hair brushing over his thick thighs before my mouth captures the hot part of him I want inside me.

I suck.

Suck the frosting off, licking his dick clean. Bob my head up and down like a pro, with plenty of saliva involved and zero teeth.

Phillip's fists attempt to grip the carpet. Reach for my hair, pulling it back so he can watch.

"Fuck, Spencer. I don't want to come like this."

I lift my head to look at his face; it's red, desire in his glassy eyes.

"What do you want?"

"I want to fuck you."

Okay then.

"Are you on the pill?"

"Yes." Thank God. And I'm getting my period any day now.

"Do you…"

"Want you to fuck me right now? Yes." I readjust on the floor, lying so we're missionary. "If I have rug burn after this, I'm going to kill you."

"Baby, you're definitely going to have rug burn, but I'll rub cream on it for you."

He's over me now and it feels familiar. Right. Not at all strange or self-conscious like I've felt with previous partners, partners I'd known longer before climbing into bed with them.

Or—spreading my legs on the living room floor.

Hard as a rock, Phillip mimics my earlier movements, sliding his hand between my legs, stroking. Finger expertly finding that nub, circling it. Pressing down, hitting that spot only I've been able to find.

One hand on my clit, the other resting on the floor, supporting him while he lavishes my body with kisses. Sucking on my nipples then blowing. I'm so hot, so burning hot.

On f-f-fire.

My hands bury themselves in his hair while he sucks on my breasts, driving me crazier with every heartbeat, learning the quickness of my breath and silent communication, the same way I will do with him.

Finally, *finally* he's hovering above me in a play that's as old as time. Kissing my mouth as he lines himself up, we make out like two teenagers hiding in the basement after prom so they're not discovered. It feels naughty and somewhat sinful to be banging on my living room floor, and I wonder if I'll sit on the couch tonight staring at this spot where my ass is reliving this encounter.

Probably.

Sex in the bedroom would be better—or sex on the table—but I'll have to settle for rug burn during this spur-of-the-moment sexcapade.

Phillip's dick is average and eases in slowly, no theatrics or ill-fitting shafts to ruin the moment—whoever said bigger is better hasn't met Joe Average. Watching his face is glorious; the range of emotions that pass over it. Euphoria. Rapture. Pleasure.

That sharp intake of breath as he slides in as deep as he can go.

He's not the only one gasping; my breath is labored from the very start, my head tipped back against the floor as he begins rotating his hips, pressing into my pelvis with his.

Deeper.

More. "More."

I'm not usually a talker, but I have faith in this budding new relationship. Miranda is going to die when I tell her how Phillip showed up at my door with a cake, got down on one knee, and proposed. She. Will. Die.

Just like I'm going to die if he doesn't go harder.

"Yeah, like that," I encourage, lifting my hips off the rug so his dick hits me where I want it most.

"You like that?" He moans, voice dipping low into my ear, through my cerebellum, straight to my pussy. Huge turn-on. Huge lady boner. "You're so tight."

If I were a peacock—and if I weren't being thoroughly fucked—I'd parade back and forth in the room, showing off, the compliment spurring me on. Filling me with pride.

I have a tight pussy?

Best compliment ever.

It makes me feel as if I've never had previous sexual partners and Phillip is the only one—because he is. He's the only one who matters, anyway.

He thrusts. I push on his ass, drawing him in closer. Boobs and chest pressed together, sweat touching skin. Breath. Chest hair. Fingers stroking in tandem. Need, want, desperation.

We dirty-talk the shit out of each other until the nerves inside my P give the telltale signs of an impending orgasm. It excites me knowing it's coming—and, desperate for it, I spread my legs wider. Hands grip Phillip's ass firmly.

"Oh shit…" he groans. "Oh f-fuck…"

Yes, yes.

"Come inside me, baby," I urge, egging him on, not wanting him to pull out. If he pulls out, I won't come. Or, I will, but it won't be the same, then I'll probably whine from post-orgasm letdown. That moment you orgasm but it's ruined? Knowing it could have felt fantastic but didn't?

God, what am I saying?

"Are you sure?"

Bad, bad girl, living on the edge.

"Yes, fuck yes, I'm coming too." *Oh God, I can feel it, I can feel it, I can feel it.*

"The mouth on you," are the last words he says before I feel him come, throbbing. Pulsing. Warm and wet.

We breathe heavy, Phillip falling onto me—I plant my hands against his chest to prevent him from crushing me.

"That was amazing," he murmurs into my shoulder.

It was.

20

PHILLIP

"I'm going to miss you at work." Spencer pushes out her bottom lip as I trace a finger down her sternum, all the way to her belly button. Move it down between our bodies, to her smooth happy trail that flirts with the neatly trimmed patch between her thighs. "You're so annoying, yet so entertaining."

I'm annoying? Me?

Was that a compliment wrapped in an insult? It's hard to tell; she delivers it with a straight face, hand brushing the stubble on my cheek lovingly.

"Same goes for you," I remind her. "When you were eating chips that first day I was in your office, I wanted to freaking strangle you. You don't even know how bad."

"Oh, I have a feeling I know how bad—the noise of that damn pencil was driving me insane." Spencer pauses, hand flopping back to the ground, and I watch her, body still splayed sexily on her beige living room floor. Her stomach growls. "Know what I want right now?"

My heads lift a fraction of an inch and I look at her. Place a kiss on the lower corner of her mouth. "Round two?"

"God no." She laughs. "More cake." I move to give her

room, and she sits up. "While I'm washing up, do you want to find some plates? We can eat in bed."

Uh, no. "We are *not* eating in bed."

"But it's my bed! And I need a nap! It says so right on the cake—cake and naps."

She is so stubborn; I hope it's not the death of me.

"Spencer, do not tell me you're the type of girl who eats chips and crackers in the bedroom."

I earn a diminutive shrug. "*All* I said was, I'm hungry and would it kill you to spoon-feed me while I leisurely lie back like an Egyptian princess sprawled out in my domain?"

"Grapes—yes. Cake—no. God, just the thought of rolling onto crumbs makes my skin crawl," I declare. But while we're on the subject of dirty things in or on or around the bed… "How do you feel about dogs on the bed?"

She doesn't blink. "Hard no."

This shocks me. She loves Humphrey! "Why?"

Spencer rises, naked as the day she was born, dimples on her ass winking at me. Waddling in the direction of the bathroom, she glances over her shoulder. "Are you telling me that dog of yours can jump onto your bed? Do you have a mattress on the floor you're not telling me about?"

"He can't jump up, no."

"Do you lift him up?" Her head peeks around a doorframe. "Or do you have one of those pet staircases next to your bed?"

"I have to lift him—if I'm feeling generous enough to let him up." He's a beggar and those brown eyes are impossible to resist about sixty percent of the time.

"That dog's belly scrapes the ground and you let him on the bed? Ew, Phillip," she calls from the bathroom.

I'm already up and in the kitchen with the cake, digging for forks. Chances are, we won't finish it anyway, so—might as well fork the damn thing.

Naked, I pad around the space, swiping two paper towels off

the roll, and pull up a chair. Sit and wait, silver fork already buried in frosting.

Spencer reappears a few minutes later with her hair in a sleek ponytail, wearing pink boy short underwear and a faded gray T-shirt. She stops short, gawking.

"Please tell me your balls are *not* on my chair."

I stick a forkful of cake in my gullet and talk with my mouth full. "My balls are not on your chair."

She plunks down beside me, face flushed. Grabs the other fork I've laid out across from me. "No dicks on the furniture! I eat breakfast there!"

"Is that a house rule? Because it should be."

"Rules get you into trouble—are you sure you want to venture into that territory?" She punctuates this statement by plopping a tiny piece of cake corner onto her tongue then biting down, frosting escaping from the side of her mouth. Like drool.

Jeez. It's a good thing I already like her, and that she's seen me at my worst—puking in the trash. I suppose I can't fault her for the slobber.

Humphrey slobbers and I still love and adore *him*.

"You're probably right about the rules, but that's not going to stop me from doing it." Old habits die hard. She'll have to train it out of me with patience and sex and letting me go down on her a few times a week.

I bet her pussy tastes better than this cake...

I'm dying to find out.

I shovel frosting into my mouth instead of vagina, and Spencer notices my deep scowl.

"What's that look on your face?"

I'm honest with her. "I want to eat you out, but we just fucked without a condom."

She reaches over with her free hand and pats my arm. "There, there, now. Don't despair. I suppose you can go down on me tonight."

"You'd really let me?" My expression is one of hope and teasing. "Don't say it if you don't mean it."

"Rule two," she states, pointing her fork into the air. "We're always honest and never make promises or threats we don't intend to follow through on. That includes me bribing you with oral, knowing I'm not going to blow you."

Shit. The promise of a blowie with no follow-through?

I visibly shudder.

Spencer laughs adorably around a mouthful. "You're so dramatic. But cute."

"And sexy?" I lean forward so she can kiss me.

She does.

"I'm thinking we should put some clothes on and take the dog for a walk?" I set the fork down and stretch, naked, ass rubbing against her chair.

Spencer's eyes trail down my torso, narrowing. "No balls on the furniture."

A kiss on her nose. "Already a stickler."

21

SPENCER

I haven't been assigned to Phillip's office.

I mean, the odds weren't that great anyway, but after deciding not to work from home (which guaranteed I wouldn't see Phillip at all), I followed my assignment to a corner office on the north side, straight to a man named Dan.

My desk is nudged snuggly against his, devoid of my clutter and computer, and any ornamentation—as is Dan's entire office.

Is he planning on quitting? The man doesn't have a single decoration, photo, or poster on his wall.

Beige and boring.

I glance out the glass wall toward the cubicles and neighboring offices, noticing a glaring similarity: those have no decorations either.

I've never been on this side, not even to run paperwork over.

I'm fascinated by the differences.

Bland office spaces. Desks and drafting tables laden with rolls of plans. Paper. Stacks of manila folders. One office has a large map displayed over the dry erase board, red tacks covering an area that must be a potential project, or one of our existing ones.

It's hard to tell from here, and I don't want to be nosey.

Sighing, I hesitate in Dan's doorway. Is it weird if I make myself at home and start unpacking my crap?

Also—where is Phillip? He wanted to take the dog out one last time before hitching a taxi to the office, but Humphrey couldn't have given him that much trouble—could he?

We spent the weekend going back and forth between each other's places, walking the dog, grabbing food. Flirting. Having sex, making out. Playing games and watching movies.

My throat is sore from laughing.

My heart is full from how sweet and caring he has been.

An ass, too—but I like it. It's not over the top, and he's not overbearing. It's the right combination of douchebag and gentleman to keep me satisfied.

The dog, on the other hand? Could use some manners.

I glance down at my phone to see a text from Phillip: *Running late. Humphrey found mud and I had to give him a quick bath.*

Me: *Are you for real?*
Phillip: *I know he's cute and all, but I'm going to lose my job because of a damn dog.*
Me: *I don't think your boss is here yet.*
Phillip: *It's not my boss I worry about. It's Paul—he loves busting my chops.*
Me: *Maybe you should bring the cake with you when you come—we can bribe him.*
Phillip: *I'm not sharing my sex cake with him. He's trying to get me written up.*
Me: *SEX cake?!*
Phillip: *Pink and sweet, like your tits.*

I blush from the roots of my hair down to the tips of my toes. No man has ever spoken to me like that and it thrills me. I stare at that word—tits.

Me: *Are you going to be able to handle being in the office with me? You sound ready for a romp.*

Phillip: *Yeah, this whole conversation is making me hard. Maybe I should rub one out before I leave the house.*

Me: *Well. Enjoy that while I'm stuck at work.*

Phillip: *We should have called in sick.*

Me: *OMG. You are a terrible influence!*

Phillip: *Did they put you in my office?*

Me: *No, I'm with some guy named Dan?*

Phillip: *Ah—he does the estimating. He'll bore you half to death, you should definitely call in sick.*

Me: *I'M ALREADY HERE.*

Phillip: *That does seem to be a problem…*

Phillip: *You should put your shit in my office and if someone is already there, tell them to go to Dan's office.*

Me: *Should I?*

Phillip: *Babe. You DEFINITELY should.*

Phillip: *100%*

Me: *Don't get any ideas about screwing around—I do not want to get caught fooling around. I would die. And we'd probably get fired.*

Phillip: *We would DEFINITLEY get fired.*

Me: *Um, okay. So which one is your office?*

Phillip: *301-3*

Me: *This feels kind of scandalous—I'm about to kick someone out.*

Phillip: *Whoever it is, they won't give a shit.*

Me: *If you say so…*

Phillip: *I do. I'll be there in 20—keep the place warm for me.*

Nervously, I do as he says, grateful that Dan hasn't arrived yet as it means I can avoid an awkward conversation about why I'm removing my things, forsaking anything in the drawers—those are taped up anyway, and nothing inside is absolutely necessary. All I need is my computer, my glasses, and my imagination.

Phillip's office is easy to locate—the floor is a giant square, offices along the wall, cubicles in the middle of the room—and I stand in its threshold, looking at the walls and ornamentation.

Unlike Dan, he has large pieces of art hanging. They're black and white photographs of skyscrapers, a pair of large framed prints centered in the middle of the room.

Black desk. Potted plant—the same one I have in my office —in the corner. One desk chair (two for guests stacked outside). Another desk is obviously pushed against his, but at least I can get a feel for his vibe without having him here, watching me scrutinize everything.

I set my things down. Pull up a chair and sit.

Twist around when an employee from the south side— Mindy Davenport—appears a few moments later, confused. "Am I in the right place?"

Mindy is in accounting, and from what I know of her, she's analytical and plays by the rules.

I push a piece of hair behind my ear and give her a megawatt smile. "You are, but if you don't mind, I'd love to use this office instead? Phillip—it's his office—he and I are friends."

Her eyes widen. "Oh! Okay, sure, no big deal, I'll just…" She's babbling, repeating herself. "I can go. No big deal."

I give her another friendly smile. "I was in Dan's office, 301-5. He's two doors down—you don't have far to go."

"Okay good. Good. Thank you."

"No—thank *you*."

She throws a wave over her shoulder, backing out, hitting the trim molding with her shoulder and giggling, clutching her folders. "Whoops."

And here I thought I was an awkward human.

Phillip keeps his promise, arriving twenty minutes after our texts ended, panting as he approaches the office—I can hear him breathing before he walks through the threshold, ever-present laptop bag in tow.

He bends and kisses the top of my head. "Morning."

He smells like wet dog.

I keep that fun factoid to myself.

"You look no worse for wear," I say instead, knowing full well he's been through the wringer with the dog this morning. In reality, his hair is sticking up in a few places. His shirt—which has come untucked a bit—has a wet spot on the front, and even though he most likely changed into a fresh one after giving Humphrey a bath, the imp managed to get him wet again anyway.

"I don't? I swear, I almost lost my damn mind this morning. I barely had time to change my clothes. The dog was in rare form."

"Where did he find mud?" In the city no less.

"Someone had been watering their plants with a hose. Humphrey caught sight and made a beeline for it. I couldn't even hold on to him. He broke free, and by the time I caught up, he was covered with planting soil." He lets out an enormous sigh. "That woman was pissed."

"I probably would be too if a giant Basset Hound came barreling at me first thing in the morning while I was tending my garden."

The fact that most plants are going dormant this time of year isn't worth mentioning; Phillip is frustrated enough already without me broaching mundane arguments.

"Bet you looked pretty cute covered in mud."

He shoots me a look. "I mean…" Shrugs. "Maybe." His eyes rake me up and down, noting the flirty, baby blue blouse that's covered in bright flowers. My large, gold hoop earrings. Wavy hair. "Bet *you* would."

"Oh, I absolutely would." I give my long hair a toss to illustrate my cuteness, letting him look.

His mouth twists, uncertain. "Maybe this was a bad idea."

"Oh, it's absolutely a bad idea." The playful banter oozes out of me like honey.

"Want to stroll with me to the breakroom? We'll get coffee."

"And a bagel? With cream cheese?"

Phillip's brow goes up, surprised. "No! God no—why would you bring that up?"

"I'm just saying—it's kind of like our anniversary today, so we should relive the first time we met."

"Or not."

I tilt my head, thinking. "How much would it take for you to eat rotten cream cheese again? On a bagel, of course."

"I threw that container away."

"I know, I know—I'm just asking how much it would take, if I paid you to eat it."

We get quiet for a few seconds as he mulls it over in his head. "Hmm," he hums. "I would eat it for…I don't know, a hundred bucks?"

"One hundred? That's it! I thought you were going to say one thousand or something. No way would I do it for so cheap. You puked, dude."

I rise so we can head to the breakroom and he watches me, disgusted.

"Well how the hell am I supposed to know?!"

"You're cheap—I like it. There's nothing wrong with that."

"Okay, I'd do it for fifteen hundred dollars."

My head shakes as we make our way down the corridor. The carpet along the way is new, and fresh, smells distinctly like floor glue and fibers. "Too late—you already said one hundred. Those are the rules."

"I can change my mind."

"No you can't."

"Who said?"

I give him an authoritative, sidelong glance. "*I* did."

"You're not the boss."

I smile. "Says who?"

He gets quiet. "God, I just want to…" He leans in closer so no one overhears him. "Fuck you right now."

He's given up so much for me—I'm more upset about him losing the baseball season tickets than he is, not to mention the ATV he has to keep in storage because there's no place to park it in the city. I would have loved to take that baby for a spin in the country, but no—he went and lost the bet.

Says he wants to date the shit out of me, and we don't need season tickets to the Jags—not when we can sit on the back deck of his house, on the tiny porch outside his bedroom, and listen to the crowds of the stadium. See its lights at night glowing in the near distance.

It all sounds so perfect, I can hardly wait for spring.

"…wearing those cute pants of yours—the black ones you wore last week that drove me out of my mind."

"I'm not banging you at work. Ever."

"Never?"

"No! It's unprofessional. Don't make me report this to Paul." I pull at the hem of his shirt that's still hanging out of the waistband of his jeans. "I'll take a rain check on that, though. Tonight, after work…"

"Do not bring his name up while I'm trying to get frisky."

"But Paul loves you now," I continue teasing.

Actually, he loves the dog; Paul is using Phillip so he can take Humphrey to the dog park. Calls the dog a Babe Magnet, one he uses to find dates from fellow dog lovers—not that Phillip cares. It gets his canine pal out of the house and out of his hair.

Unreal.

"You were saying?" He nudges. "Tonight after work…?"

He lets the sentence trail off so I have to get closer still. So close I have to whisper my answer.

"Tonight after work? You can bang the rules into me then."

EPILOGUE

HUMPHREY

"Humphrey, come."

I wait a few seconds before twitching my ears, having heard the command the first two times Girl firmly gave them.

It's never good to appear too eager, so I lower my eyes to the ground, feigning indifference.

Three.

Two.

One.

"Humphrey. *Come.*"

Finally, I happily go, lumbering to her enthusiastically, knowing Girl is going to drop a treat in my food bowl for listening the third time.

She loves me so much, but who doesn't?

"I cannot believe that dog listens to you. It's really annoying." I can hear Boy grumbling intermittently above me as Girl kisses and pets my head. "You and Paul, his new best friend."

I do love Paul, the Boy at Boy's work, who met us at the dog park one weekend with his snotty Chihuahua, Justin Beaver. Justin might have been yippy, but Paul makes up for it with lots of pets, and Bacon YumYums.

Those are my favorite.

"What have I been telling you? All you have to do is use a commanding tone with him. He respects that." Girl likes to rub in her dog-whispering success on the occasions I refuse to follow Boy's directions, which is most of the time.

"You had to tell him three times—I thought you said it should only take one."

"I know." Girl laughs. "But he's just getting used to me. You've had five years to teach him manners."

Manners? What are manners?

I pant, saliva dripping from my tongue, down to the floor.

"Ugh, I have to grab a paper towel from the kitchen—your new best friend is drooling." Boy groans.

She's been living with us since the snow came, since the big tree got put up in the front room. Boy hasn't had a tree since I was a puppy and yanked the bottom ornaments off it, destroyed half of them with my mighty puppy jaws.

That big tree? It's real.

And I knocked it down last week.

Give me a break! Like I was supposed to know the tree would tip over—maybe if I'd known, I wouldn't have crawled underneath it for a nap. And maybe I wouldn't have gone under it for a drink from the water trough so conveniently located at its trunk.

What a fuss that caused, everyone shouting and screeching when the tree fell, smashing through the front window.

Such a ruckus. Humans overreact to *every*thing.

Sheesh.

The window was hardly a big deal—the plastic and duct tape over the shattered glass took care of it in a jiffy. I don't know what all the cursing was for.

On and on he went about "little bastard...couldn't have picked a colder day to be an asshole...cost a fucking fortune... look at him sleeping...gonna take him to boarding school... always does this..."

I don't know who Boy was talking about, but I'm glad it wasn't me. He sure did sound mad.

If you don't want the tree to topple over, make sure there's ample room under it for a Basset Hound, that's all I'm saying.

The worst part about that whole thing? Neither of them would let me lick their faces when they were on their hands and knees cleaning up the shiny balls scattered around the floor. They put me in the laundry room and shut the door while they swept glass and taped the window.

Then, when a man in a big white van came to replace the entire piece, I couldn't play with him, either. *And* I heard Boy make a few tasteless jokes about the window man taking me with him when he left.

Rude.

Girl attaches the leash to my collar, but after she's done and gone from the room, Boy bends down and scratches behind my ears. *It's about damn time.* Wipes the slobber from the hardwood floor with a white rag.

"Be a good boy for me, now, Humphrey. I'm giving you a job to do." In his hand is a small black pouch. He ties it to my collar with a ribbon then stands back to survey his handiwork. "Handsome boy." Pets me a bit more. "Be a good boy."

I pant and whine, dripping more drool on the floor.

Girl enters the room again, shrugging into a jacket so we can take our afternoon walk around the block. "Ready?"

"Ready as we'll ever be," Boy says, taking my lead and going through the front door, tree twinkling in the background, missing half the pretty balls that were there when they first decorated it.

I lumber out the door. Down the steps, the little pouch around my neck annoying me.

I stop in the middle of the sidewalk to scratch at it.

"No, Humphrey," Boys tells me, and maybe I'm wrong, but he sounds a bit panicked.

We walk on. Walk and walk and walk until I'm bored and

uninterested, the white snow cold and damp beneath my paws. With it piled high along the sidewalk, there isn't much to see from this vantage point, few tree trunks to piss on. Just cars and dirty curbs and garbage cans lining the street.

I sit.

"Come, Humphrey. We're not there yet." Boy gives me a gentle tug.

Meh.

Not interested.

Ahead of us, Girl laughs. "He's so the boss of you," she teases.

"No he's not," Boy says. "You are."

"Aww, babe!" Girl doubles back toward us and moves her face close to his, pursing her lips and kissing the tip of his snout.

"It's true."

I pant, the cold air and my warm breath creating small puffs of steam I'm suddenly fascinated with.

I lick the air, trying to catch it.

"What on earth is he doing?" Girl asks. "What a weirdo—I think he's licking his breath."

"He's a weirdo alright, but now he's your dog, too, so—not all my problem."

Girl coos again. "Keep trying to butter me up…"

I shake my head, the pouch around my neck jangling, slapping against my long, floppy ears. Like a fly buzzing around my head, it's causing constant irritation, and I shake my head again. Again.

Scratch.

"Something is bothering him," Girl observes, getting down on one knee to grasp both sides of my face and stare at my mug. "What's wrong, Humphrey?"

As if I'm going to open my mouth and tell her, *This pouch is making me crazy—get it off.*

I avert my gaze while she ogles me, not liking to look

directly into anyone's eyes. I also don't like being photographed. Or peeing on fire hydrants—that's a total myth.

"What's this?" Girl fingers the pouch dangling from my neck.

I shake it.

"Humphrey, stop," she tells me. I don't stop.

"Need help?" Boy asks, kneeling beside her, hands coming to untie the ribbon securing the pouch. He loosens it easily, tugging it free and palming it.

Girl stands, staring down at us both, adorable me and Boy, who is on bended knee, removing a black box from the black pouch.

"What…" Girl looks perplexed. *Sounds* perplexed.

"Spencer," Boy is saying, and I'm all—*Who the hell is Spencer?* "I know we haven't known each other long, but it feels like I've known you for my entire life. I've never regretted quitting the Bastard Bachelor Society for a second, and I would do it again in a heartbeat."

"Oh my God, Phillip," she says breathlessly, and I'm all —*Who the hell is Phillip?* "What are you doing?" Her hands fly to her mouth.

Yeah Boy, what are you doing? It's cold down here. Maybe you should stand up—you're making an ass of yourself.

Get to the point so we can go home.

I bark.

"Humphrey and I love you. We couldn't imagine our life without you."

I can imagine my life without her just fine, thank you very much. Since she moved in, I'm not allowed on the bed.

"The minute I saw you, I knew."

Girl tilts her head—she does that a lot when she's being cheeky. "Oh really? You knew when you were throwing up that I was your soul mate?"

"Are you trying to make me lose my train of thought here?"

"No, I'm sorry." She zips her lips. "Don't stop." Bounces on her back feet anxiously. "Go."

"Spencer Victoria Standish, would you make me the happiest man in the world and be my wife?"

"Can we serve pink cake and chips at the wedding?"

That sounds disgusting.

"Yes." Boy flips the top of the black box up and extends it toward her, a loud gasp escaping her lips.

"Phillip! Oh my God, Phillip—it's so beautiful!"

I grunt, bored.

Shake my collar again so they know I'm serious about it, hit Boy's elbow. With a loud scream from Girl, the black box goes flying through the air, landing in a nearby snowbank.

"Holy shit!" Boy yells, lunging for the box, releasing my leash.

Freedom! Sweet freedom!

I seize the opportunity, turning toward home, and jog down the sidewalk from whence we came.

"Humphrey!" they both shout, frantically digging through the snow, torn.

"You run and grab him—I'll find the ring!" Boy tells her, and I hear her behind me, giving chase.

A chase, a chase—I love a good chase!

I speed up.

"Humphrey, no! Bad dog," she cries. "Heel! Bad dog. Stop!"

I run and run and run because, as it turns out...

I am the boss.

ABOUT THE AUTHOR

Sara Ney is the USA Today Bestselling Author of the How to Date a Douchebag series, and is best known for her sexy, laugh-out-loud New Adult romances. Among her favorite vices, she includes: iced latte's, historical architecture and well-placed sarcasm. She lives colorfully, collects vintage books, art, loves flea markets, and fancies herself British.

For more information about Sara Ney and her books, visit:
Facebook
Twitter
Website
Instagram
Books + Main
Subscribe to Sara's Newsletter
Facebook Reader Group: Ney's Little Liars

Made in the USA
Middletown, DE
24 April 2020